To
Carolyn—
Whose guiding light is
the beacon for so many, and
illumination for Mich-genis
literary showcase...
Best Bersark,
Shelly

Norman Spll

August 20, 1999

THE MARTYRING

THE MARTYRING

THOMAS SULLIVAN

A TOM DOHERTY ASSOCIATES BOOK
New York

THE MARTYRING

Copyright © 1998 by Thomas Sullivan

This book is printed on acid-free paper.

A Forge Book
Published by Tom Doherty Associates, Inc.
175 Fifth Avenue
New York, NY 10010

Forge® is a registered trademark of Tom Doherty Associates, Inc.

Design by Helene Berinsky

Library of Congress Cataloging-in-Publication Data

Sullivan, Thomas.
    The martyring / Thomas Sullivan. —1st ed.
      p.   cm.
    "A Tom Doherty Associates book."
    ISBN 0-312-86361-6
    I. Title.
  PS3569.U3579M3   1998
  813'.54—dc21   97-29853
                                  CIP

First Edition: March 1998

Printed in the United States of America

0 9 8 7 6 5 4 3 2 1

For Loren D. Estleman, ink bro.
The indelible kind.

ACKNOWLEDGMENTS

My gratitude to Win Blevins for the consummate editing skill that only another writer could provide. And special thanks to Kathleen McBroom, for performing her usual role of muse in my career, as well as to Fred Bean, creator of the world's first edible cremation.

THE MARTYRING

ONE

FALL, 1976

THAT LAST MORNING in Germany he never said a word to his mother. He couldn't. It was as if they were already an ocean apart, and he was watching her on film, her gray head scarcely definable from all that steam in the kitchen. Nobody made more steam than his mother. The hissing offerings of ten thousand meals. None of them cold.

She swung down like a well-oiled hinge to peer into the oven now, poked at the slices of white bread bubbling with butter, skewered them one after another, and swung them onto the table like decked, compliant fish. Her rapid tiny steps took her to the cupboard and back again carrying a chipped saucer filled with syrup. Then she brisked about on the same roller-bearing gait, gathering juice, pitcher, napkin, coffee, and with a final maternal flourish two yellow vitamin pills.

His sister watched him with dusky jealousy. "So that's what you look like with your hair combed."

It was the last arrow she would ever shoot at him, and his pale blue irises deflected it.

11

Ursa wiped her gnarled hands. "Don't tease, Monika. It's good that he wants to impress Uncle Martin. They'll all see what his intentions are, and that he'll be a good worker." Moving back to the sink to rinse the broiler pan, she added: "America. Even your father never got that far."

Comparison with his father pleased Kurt. As a manufacturer's representative, Karl Nehmer had traveled freely throughout Europe before his death on a trip in and out of East Germany two years earlier. In and out. Significant prepositions. One did not go "to" and "from" East Germany but "in" and "out." A border delay in getting his father to a West German hospital after the car accident had hastened death. And the sudden loss had cut Kurt adrift, because he wasn't ready to anchor a family of women. He wanted to belong, not to lead. He had grown up with a sense of exile, of remoteness from the true center of their family. The Nehmer history dead-ended with his father, because Karl Nehmer had been an orphan; and here were the family albums and the picture frames on the walls burgeoning with Hauptmanns. The dishes, the books, and the bric-a-brac were Hauptmann legacies from his mother's girlhood, and she had a lifetime supply of Hauptmann familial anecdotes or associations that covered any event. Nehmer was a name, but Hauptmann was a river of blood. And now Kurt was going to America, like an emissary from his mother, schooled and mandated to belong.

But he didn't feel like he was going to belong. The Hauptmann men were skilled craftsmen by the time they were twenty, while he had no training at all in the art of making stained glass.

"Aunt Anna will be delighted," Ursa went on. "And Gerta, what grandmother can resist a handsome, seventeen-year-old grandson? Grandmamma has never seen any of the boys. Neither Hans nor Otto. She'll burst when she sees Kurt."

"She'll spoil him," Monika said dryly.

"Not Grandmamma. She never spoiled any of us. It was Papa who did the spoiling. Old Grandfather Josef. He never saw any of his grandchildren. He died the year Anna and Martin married, the year Eva-Marie had Hans and I had you."

"What about Ute? You didn't mention how impressed *she* will be with Kurt."

Kurt tongued a syrupy wedge of bread off the roof of his mouth. "Oh, yes, yes," he said. "I'm in love with my cousin."

"Don't talk with your mouth full, little brother."

"Enough. In a little while our young man will be going, Monika. God willing, we'll see him again, but I don't know when."

Making a mock toast, Kurt collected the vitamins and downed his mother's last double dose of health. "Well," he declared, and the word was like an engine turning over. The sound of it frightened him, though he tried to look resolute.

At once Ursa began to wipe her hands, nod, swallow, blink away tears. Monika assumed a crisp look.

"You have your cross on, don't you, son? You'll wear it as you promised?"

He produced the ebony icon, twin to his sister's.

"If you sleep on the plane, you'll wear it, please, for your silly old mother."

He nodded.

"Good. Now I'm happy. Now I can see you go. Monika, run and tell Herr Schultz your brother is ready to go to the airport."

Monika threw on her navy jacket against the November cold as she went out the door and swung quickly round the white picket fence. Narrow two-story houses formed descending steps down the slicing road. The third of these was distressed brick with wooden gateposts. In the modest drive that brushed the doorstep sat a lemon yellow Volkswagen. Her knock brought Herr Schultz outside immediately, already swathed in a tan woolen scarf.

"Yes, yes, it's time!" he perceived, brushing streusel from his mustache. Snatching his coat, he heel-and-toed round to the driver's side.

Monika rode the fifty feet or so up the street to where Kurt struggled at the fence with the venerable old portmanteau. Ursa bobbed forward then to plant the final kiss, and that picturesque benediction done, Herr Schultz eased the car into gear.

When the white exhaust had vanished frenetically up the street, Ursa felt along her collar for the little black crucifix around her own neck. Holding it against her lips, she whispered a brief prayer. "Let Martin teach him to be a Hauptmann," she said. "And may he never be tested." Then the wind stirred her graying forelock and she followed Monika inside.

▪ ▪ ▪

HE TOOK THE planes—a Lufthansa to Heathrow, a Pan Am to Miami International—zigzagging his way to America, and the long final flight gave him too much time to think. He was building a bridge across an ocean, he told himself, a bridge across time, across families, but what if he really didn't fit in at the studio? What if they thought his English was funny? What if he couldn't get along with Ute? The only grown-up Hauptmann he had ever met was Uncle Detlef, and that had been an unqualified disaster. It had happened when he was six or seven, a pilgrimage to Chartres with his cousin Otto and his uncle. He could not remember the details, just that he had displeased Detlef, and that afterward he had cried and wouldn't tell his mother about the journey for fear of disappointing her. There was a stained-glass pane next to the breakfast nook at home. It had been sent from

America by Uncle Martin in his youth. In winter, the morning sun would catch it just right, setting the mosaic of colors afire. "That piece is Grandmamma, and that one Ute," his mother would say. She had a family name for each fragment. But there was an odd piece, pale yellow against the spectrum of reds and blues, and less symmetrically shaped, which she never named. That was for him, he thought. Kurt Nehmer. Not really part of the pattern. Just filling up space.

The sun on the ocean below struck stained-glass motifs now, as if it were a trail he must follow, and he peered anxiously out to the horizon as the big Pan Am began its final descent. America! He wasn't ready for this. His fingers played absently over the beginnings of a beard. How could he have ever thought this would work? And then Miami International was rising up like a pink and white desert, and he became distracted by the landing protocols.

He got his first look at subtropic fauna and flora through the sea green lozenges of a Greyhound bus. There were snowy birds, immobile on single reed legs, and the unarranged beauty of cypress draped with lime-hued streamers of Spanish moss. The number of stucco and cinder-block houses surprised him. Like a roll of Alka 2, projecting cannonlike off a sign on a curve, they seemed "built to fall apart." Was this affluent America? At last the plain emerald road sign he was looking for emerged: Marlo County. And twenty minutes later, out of the rapidly gathering darkness, there was Padobar.

His first step off the hermetically sealed bus acquainted him with agreeable things within the shadows of the town. Orange sodium lights along the highway shed a gold graininess over the horizontal planes of a tightly clustered corner, turning it into a daguerreotype. Hoisting the portmanteau, he ambled into the Stop 'n' Go convenience store at hand for directions to the Hauptmann studio.

"Guess you mean the stained-glass place," said the female clerk. "Just down the road. Chapel Lane. Turn right."

The night chirred with insect voices that seemed to stay ahead of him. Chapel Lane . . . Chapel Lane. The next crossroad was dirt, and the next. Then he came to sandy ruts faintly luminescent between twin lines of firs. He had to bend down to read the metal sign leaning against the wood post: Chapel Lane. Pinecones and toads dotted the fine sand at his feet, and finally a rabbit—judging by its broken hops—brought his eyes up to the compound.

To the left was a small orchard, to the right a long black shed. A lighted window peered from the second story of another, undefinable structure. At his next step, something poured out of the darkness of the shed. It came straight at him, then turned at his feet, brushing the leg opposite the portmanteau. He bent and stroked the back and tail of a corpulent cat.

At second glance, the undefinable structure resolved itself into a building like a church pew, narrow upper story indented above the first. Within the soaring top wedge were a series of tightly hemmed rectangles that glittered like troubled water. The studio, of course. Inside would be the heart of the family: countless centuries of glassmaking art. It was smaller than he had imagined, simpler than Anna's letters portrayed. But then, the Hauptmanns had never been materialists. Had they been wealthy, no outsider would have known.

He turned up the wooden steps of the house, and shadows immediately flitted across the window. Beneath his knuckles the flimsy door frame sent a repercussive buzz through the screen. A seam of light slowly broadened and a very old face hung a little below his.

"Yes?" She had short, salt 'n' pepper brows that drooped like hoary parentheses. Her skin was quilted and her hair was white.

"Grandmamma?"

The salt 'n' pepper brows arched; the eyes—vivid points suddenly—darted to the portmanteau. "Kurt?"

She embraced him with improbable strength as he came across the threshold, and from over her shoulder he caught the stunned expressions of a handful of figures rising. The heavy woman with the puffy face and rust-colored hair was his Aunt Anna, he was sure. And Ute Margit. Lithe, comely, green eyes, reddish hair, a strong, knowing face. Ute, no question about it. Another woman, somber, perhaps Anna's age, stood beside a somber man, hat in hand, who could not be Uncle Martin. They stood stiffly, as if they did not belong here, did not want to be here.

"Child . . . child," Gerta cooed. "I'm afraid we simply forgot you."

"Uncle Martin wrote that I should call when I got in. But it wasn't far to walk."

The awkwardness extended to everyone now. He noticed that Anna's eyes were red-rimmed.

"Child," Gerta repeated more firmly, "your uncle is dead."

TWO

HE HAD DIED precisely as Kurt's plane was setting down at Miami International. Something gained, something lost. Gerta would think of that. But Jack Skelote had no premonition of what was about to unfold in Marlo County, or the enormity of its roots across two continents and twenty centuries.

He saw the body before they put it in the ambulance. Knew the man was dead. No two of these old codgers died alike. Some of them had rigor mortis before they hit the floor.

"It's Hauptmann, Lieutenant," someone said.

"Yeah," Skelote acknowledged. *Martin B. Hauptmann,* he jotted down in his notebook. "Anyone see it?"

A score of shoppers outside the Publix market looked eager. Skelote nodded and let it drop. When old folks croaked in Padobar, there were always witnesses. The corpse-elect did it for effect. It would make the Wednesday edition. Thirty-five hundred candidates for the next heart attack would feel reassured to know that official notice was instantly available in the geriatric capital of the South.

Out on Route 54 a siren caterwauled, and at his elbow a

woman with two fifty-pound bags of No-Brand dog food in her cart held out a metal hide-a-key box. "He dropped this, Officer."

Skelote slid the metal lid back. There was a pill inside.

"He took one," the woman said.

Skelote fished it out between his fingers. It looked too big for nitroglycerin. It looked like baby aspirin.

The crowd was starting to get bored. Probably someone had tried CPR. Probably they had done it wrong. Everyone in Padobar had taken CPR, and no one ever got it right. They pounded dying bellies, sealed mouths, and blew in nostrils. Now and then someone recovered despite first aid and sued. Nobody wanted to pose for pictures anymore. Particularly if the victim lived.

The siren on Route 54 tore into the parking lot, and the young patrolman at the wheel of a cruiser burst out of the driver's seat before the suspension stopped rocking. He wore a look of restrained eagerness, a scavenger look that Skelote had grown to detest. With his globular sunglasses on, young Catherton always reminded the lieutenant of a well-groomed housefly.

"Holdup?" Catherton demanded.

"Five men and a woman took the supermarket manager hostage and killed a cashier," Skelote monotoned. "They raped a shopper and pistol-whipped the stock boy. Then they took two point three million dollars out of the safe and fled to the parking lot. We shot it out. It's all over. Except for that." He waved at the departing ambulance. "One of the witnesses had a coronary. Someone has to tell his family. It was Martin Hauptmann. Why don't you go out to that stained-glass place and inform the next of kin? They're taking him to Palm Hollow Emergency. He'll be D.O.A., but you don't say that."

Catherton gave him a goggle-eyed, papier-mâché, fly look and asked dryly if that was all.

"No. Your holster is unsnapped. And turn off your flasher before you get there."

Catherton slunk back to his car, turned off the festivities, and eased off the lot.

"Kind of hard on the boy, weren't you?" said the woman with the dog food. There was a lazy taunt in her voice and she was looking at Skelote sideways.

He gave her a smile and was back in his own car before it occurred to him that he had just received a flirtatious look. There was a blanched circle on his ring finger atop the wheel. The divorce had been final two months ago, but he hadn't taken the ring off until last week.

He looked at himself in the rearview mirror, removed his cap, palmed back silvering hair the shade of fifty. He had aged elegantly enough. With a haircut and a little more sleep, he might pass for the captain of a stately ocean liner, eyes the color of limes tinged red from reading sunsets. But he didn't get much sleep anymore, and what the mirror said was "puffy-faced, tired cop."

The woman was still watching as he drove past. He sized her up. Flaxen hair cut short, eyes like frost on stone, a body with tone, and a face that had majesty you had to reach forty to achieve. And in the market for No-Brand dog food. Skelote burned rubber out of the lot.

▪ ▪ ▪

HE DIDN'T THINK about Hauptmann again until Thursday when the lab report came back on the pill that looked like baby aspirin. It said it was baby aspirin.

THREE

UTE KNEW THE moment she awoke that the cawing in the orchard was for her father. Grandmamma said the crows always came the day of a funeral. She swung herself out of bed and stretched as she cast a melancholy look at herself in the door-length mirror. Sophia Loren today, she decided.

Italian women impressed her. So strong and bold. Like Grandmamma. And she herself was like Grandmamma (and totally unlike her mother). Someday she would be the matriarch of the craft, the living repository of all the family lore. She knew this already. An odd ambition for so young a woman, but she was steeped in genealogy and fascinated by the extraordinary oneness of the Hauptmann identity. For her it was not actually the craft so much as family loyalty. Stained glass was more than a worship of God, it was a sanctifying of their essence. The men would take care of the craft, but the women would take care of the men.

And she knew she was romanticizing Gerta. If the test really came in her generation, it would strain the limits of everyone's sensibilities. Yet that was what they prepared for—and she more diligently than anyone else.

The clunk of a shoe alerted her to her cousin on the other side of the wall. Though he bore the name Nehmer, he had seemed very much a Hauptmann to her, quiet to the point of diffidence. He had politely offered to return home in view of the circumstances and just as quietly made no pretense when Anna and Gerta waved the thought away. Neither had he tried to impress William Mackey when they spoke briefly, even after Grandmamma said that Mackey was a master craftsman. And he was devout. That had surfaced later. After the Mackeys left, Gerta had asked him to pray with them. They had all sensed it then. God-fearing. She heard him cross the floor now, unlatch the casement. Pulling her slip on, she went to her own window.

He was looking at the chapel rising out of the trees in the other direction. The mist hung in blue wreaths on the long pine needles there; a half-dozen stained-glass windows glittered bejeweled on the near side high above the ground. It was where the studio displayed its finest work and, more importantly, where the family preserved its covenant with God.

"There are six more on the other wall," she got out before Kurt swung around, hitting his head on the sash. "Twelve altogether. One for each apostle."

"Apostle," he repeated, trying to pretend he hadn't hurt himself. Looking straight ahead, he asked, "What's that?"

"That? The studio, of course."

"And that?" He pointed halfheartedly.

"A propane tank."

"And that?"

His gaze traveled past her until she turned the other way. A green awning sat on the family plot. But he wasn't looking at the family plot.

"Those are my breasts," she said without turning back.

She didn't need the intuitive chill on her thinly veiled nipples to tell her that his hot little mind had retreated.

▪   ▪   ▪

SHE WAS DRESSED in midnight blue for the funeral, unlike Anna or Gerta who wore bustly black silk. Sunlight streamed through the east stained-glass windows of the chapel, spangling three of the six pews. Her father lay on the bier, half in light, half in darkness. At the end of the service the bell in the tower tolled once.

From chapel to grave she extracted nothing from the minister's liturgical murmur save the obtrusive dictum, "Martin Bruno Hauptmann," like a final flash of lightning connecting her father with the storms of his life. The introduction of his name and the consecration of his flesh thus flickered briefly and went out. Down coffin!

Anna and Gerta led the way back, leaning on each other, with Ute and Kurt a few paces behind. The Mackeys and Jimmy Pelt, Martin's studio artist of long-standing, hung still farther behind like pilot fish. At the porch the procession stopped and Gerta turned to speak.

"The Hauptmanns have never believed in postponing the business of living," she said. "Anna has not yet said what she will do with the studio, but we will decide soon and you will be told."

We will decide. Already the personal pronouns of power were bumping against each other. Martin had been a quiet island. By the laws of the state, Anna was his heir. By the laws of the family, that was not so clear. Anna stood there on the porch in her black veil and made no addition to Gerta's statement.

She spent the next four and a half hours of widowhood in her room before emerging quietly to prepare dinner. Gerta, who ordinarily would have helped, let her be. There were no tears. And the meal, like all the dinners to follow, was an institution of Hauptmann life in the old European manner. In a formal, joyless way it was the high point of each day. The time of coming together.

A space had been made for Kurt alongside Ute on one side of the heavy oak table. Martin's place at the head remained empty. They ate in silence. Kurt chewed like a metronome, Anna sipped wine disinterestedly, Ute shredded each morsel into oblivion with her fork. Gerta was the only one who seemed to relish the meal, and it was she who ended the pretenses when she dabbed her puckered lips with a napkin and held her goblet aloft.

"To Martin," she purred resonantly, "son, husband, father . . . uncle. May his work carry on." They all drank, and then she said: "Time past is time lost. Anna, you must tell us now what will become of the studio. Do you have the will to carry on, or have you had enough?"

The sting of that showed, even on Ute's cheeks.

Anna's voice and eyelids fluttered as, like a time-worn phoenix, she tried to rise from the ashes of her grief. "Enough?" she repeated thickly. "The craft is my life just as much as it is to someone born into this family. There is nothing to decide about the studio. You shouldn't have let the Mackeys and Jimmy think otherwise."

The old matriarch was too pleased to be ruffled by the chastisement. "You *are* a Hauptmann," she concurred. "And the craft will live to the last Hauptmann breath. But there are things to be decided about the studio, Anna. Neither you nor I nor Ute can properly head it. We aren't masters like Martin was. There are only women here now, and that is half a loaf. Perhaps in time young Kurt here will be ready. But we need a working master now . . . especially now."

"What is there that a woman can't manage?" Anna scoffed.

"It isn't the managing. Hauptmann women have always managed effectively. It's . . . *preparedness.*"

Signals and cues were flying round the table. Kurt, pleased only a moment before at her mention of him, had the feeling that he had become an obstacle to the conversation.

Anna licked her lips and seemed to consider whether she should challenge that. "And where do we turn for a master?" she breathed reluctantly at last.

"There is only one. Detlef."

Stony silence. Detlef. Martin's brother. Gerta's other son. Again Kurt had the dim recollection of something that was already old in his young life. The pilgrimage to Chartres with Uncle Detlef. Why had they gone?

"Forgive my being blunt, but Detlef is never sober long enough to manage his own life," Anna said.

Gerta nodded. "Things went downhill for him after Eva-Marie died. He never was a strong man morally—left to his own designs. But it was a different story when Eva-Marie had her hand on his shoulder. Love makes all the difference in a man like Detlef. And the stained glass he turned out in the early days! Even Martin was jealous. He had purpose then. A man without purpose strays easily, Anna."

"What makes you think he'll find purpose here?"

Detlef's "golden period" between cardinal sin and alcoholism did not precisely correspond to the entry and exit of Eva-Marie from his life, as Anna remembered. He had always struck her as having a congenital wildness that might take expression in brilliantly soaring pieces of art or in the basest vices. His canting voice forever alternated in her memory between classical High German and the crudest obscenities.

"I can't promise he'll find purpose here," Gerta said. "It may depend on how much we need him."

"He didn't respond much to the needs of Otto or Hans," Anna persisted. Detlef's two sons had grown up despite him after their mother died.

"And yet they are fine boys. There are things about Detlef I don't even know. Who can say how tender the thunderstorm is to a thirsty flower?"

Anna didn't find this analogy the least reassuring, yet she doubted that Detlef could harm the studio. At worst he would simply fail to be an asset. Otto and Hans on the other hand—

"How providential that we are three generations of Hauptmann women who have lost the protection of our men, and they are three Hauptmann men who have lost the guidance of their women, don't you think?" Gerta's math seemed to exclude Kurt.

"I'll write Detlef tomorrow," Anna said.

FOUR

DETLEF BRENEMANN HAUPTMANN swarmed up the church roof over the north arm of the transept and found a foothold near the junction of the nave. His elder son, twenty-one-year-old Hans, crouched terrified above the triforium. An eye-wrenching infinity below, eighteen-year-old Otto watched apprehensively.

"Climb, Hans; a steeplejack welcomes heights!" Detlef flung himself up the slippery tiles to the apex, there to stand grinning atop the rooftree. "It's his freedom. Spread your wings and soar!"

Hans glanced from the tiny vent cowling his father had pushed off of to the precipitous drop and licked his lips. "Don't look down!" he heard from above, like a celestial commandment. He closed his eyes but couldn't stop the vertigo.

"You won't fall," scoffed Detlef. "This church is God's thimble. You'll climb both towers of Elizabethkirche in Marburg before you die!"

Somehow Hans got through these occasional jobs steeple-jacking, somehow survived by clinging frantically to every line and support within reach. But this was higher than he had ever been, steeper. *Never again,* he vowed to himself. *Never, never, never—*

The dreadful measured slick of tiles startled him. His father slithered toward him, ending in a dramatic rush that made Hans brace himself for a collision. He felt the old man's fishy breath and, somehow, the abrasiveness of his grizzled face. The voice, which had been beveled flat by too many drinks and too many cigarettes, could still ring like a cold chisel when his father steeple-jacked and something transcendent entered him. Hans felt its icy bite powdering his will.

"If you don't trust your father, trust God. I've climbed Strasbourg and Bamberg and Cologne. Gothic is steep, it defies gravity, it flies! If you trust it, it will carry you aloft. Faith, Hans. Only unbelievers plummet to the ground."

"It's too steep."

"This bit of church that isn't fit to be the apse of a cathedral? Look at it. Built on a budget to the glory of God. Perpendicular windows—the kind the English made—with more paint than fire in them." He shot up enraged, his mouth flecked, his speech a bawdy mix of High German and slang as he pulled Hans to his feet. "Follow me, and remember, if you don't attack, the roof will resist you. Throw yourself up the same as you would a parish roof."

"Can't we use the hooks?"

"Hooks? We'll use hooks when we get to the towers."

With that, he sprang lightly off the vent cowl, pushing sideways rather than down on the steep transept roof. He seemed to flow laterally to the rooftree again.

Knowing delay might be fatal, Hans wet his lips and sprang. And for a moment he believed. But his initial leap was too far up the roof to keep his feet under him. He compacted stiffly and made a single awkward twist—too late, too high. The last rational picture he saw in that insane sequence was his father, arms outstretched against the running sky. Faith, Hans, fly with me! Spread your wings and soar. The unbeliever slid and scraped interminably before plunging to the ground.

■　■　■

ANNA'S LETTER ARRIVED six days after Hans's death. Otto brought it in and tossed the envelope on the table.

"Read it to me," Detlef said.

Otto wanted to read it, but they hadn't spoken since the funeral. It was a small enough protest on his part. How else could he tell his father that he held him to blame? How else to let him know that he didn't want to inherit the meager love that had been reserved for his older brother alone? His mother's childbirth death had insured that.

"Read it yourself," he said about the letter.

"Don't be insolent, Otto. I'm down to one son, and he's going to grow up right." The ether of invincibility that invested his father above the vaults and squinches of Gothic temples seemed to have followed him to the ground, and when his eyes were not haunted, they were reckless. They were reckless now.

"You killed your only son."

His father would have grabbed him then, if he had been sober enough to catch him. But Detlef only rose up ominously, saw the irony of losing control, and softened.

"Come now, Otto, let's put this aside. It's not the time for blame. If blame would bring your brother back, I'd go down on my knees."

Otto was beginning to wheeze, his asthma rising with his emotions.

"Do you think it was easy, raising two sons by myself?" Detlef continued. "Your mother had all the graces. Give me credit for not pretending I could do what she did. If you'd known her, you'd understand what was lost and why things were the way they were. Don't blame me for that. How can you blame *me* for that?"

"You're the one who fixed the blame."

He should have taken the gesture, weak as it was. His father had never offered anything conciliatory before, drunk or sober. But in the pain and fear following his brother's death, he could not. The fear was because the wolf pack code that had kept them together for survival had ended with Hans.

But the letter . . . Otto didn't see that right away. Detlef read it, mumbled over it, kept it with himself for two days. And he was reading it again that evening when he fell asleep drinking. As his breathing deepened, Otto reached gingerly over his arm to press the paper smooth with splayed fingers. Thus, he learned of his Uncle Martin's death and of the invitation to America. Anna was blunt about drinking. And they would be expected to show good deportment, as Kurt Nehmer was presently doing. Suddenly the hand alongside Otto's came to life.

"Luckier for you if I had died and your mother lived!" hissed at him, and the fist tightened with enormous strength around his throbbing wrist.

"Luckier for Hans, too," Otto said, forcing his voice smooth.

Detlef's strength withered and became merely human. "Hans died a man."

"I knew you never loved me."

Sodden eyes rolled up as if fighting to raise steel shutters, willing something at him. And then Detlef's whole face began to quiver, and the shutters turned gray.

"We're going," he said. "That's what I'm reduced to. But before we go, I want it finished between us. Hans slipped off that roof. It was his mistake. If you believe to the contrary, say so now." The wind gusted against the window, setting the three spheres of the rotary pendulum adrift on the broken mantel clock. "Good then. We won't carry our dead to America."

FIVE

BABY ASPIRIN.

Martin Hauptmann's doctor said he was supposed to be carrying something called Nitrostat antianginal to save his life, but he was carrying baby aspirin instead. What for? Tiny headaches? Where was the nitro?

At this point in his career, Skelote could recognize a Pandora's box while it was still unopened. There were things you left alone, because they didn't really need investigating, even though you knew everything didn't fit. Like old men having heart attacks in front of twenty witnesses. If you tried to figure out everyone's quirks, you became Alice in Wonderland. People carried baby aspirin instead of breaking up adult tablets. They kept nitroglycerin and aspirin in hide-a-key boxes instead of the nice clean glass ones with the life-saving instructions on them; and they got them mixed up. Quirks. Leave them alone. The missing nitro was in Pandora's box.

And if you *were* going to play Sherlock with this one, you went to see the man's widow who was ten years younger and maybe got tired of keeping him alive. Not the woman with the cheap dog

32

food. The woman with the cheap dog food was a tease. When you finally found her, all you could say would be, "Oh, yeah?" Just looking for her would mean that you were lonely for a woman and that your life was wasting away. Skelote didn't think about his life wasting away, but he felt like one of those bugs that only live for twenty-four hours and it was raining on his day.

She lived in a trailer park and her name was Nora Sandles. She had a basset that looked like it ate moldy dog food by the twenty-five-pound bagful. Skelote found her on his third pass down the street. Actually there weren't that many places a woman in her circumstances could live in Padobar. She was hanging up sheets and the basset lay on the lawn like it had just worn the last of its legs down to nothing.

He ambled out of the car and confronted her. "Nice, dog," he said.

He wasn't looking at the dog. The sheets were flapping and she was studying him sideways again. "You don't like dogs, Lieutenant," she said.

Lieutenant. The other day she had called him Officer. He had thought that she couldn't read his stripes. Maybe she had taken the trouble to learn.

"How do you know I don't like dogs?"

"Because you don't like people."

He glanced at the dead sausage on the lawn. It glanced back. Sideways, like her. Lots of white around the eye.

"I like dogs. I like some people."

She sucked her cheek. "That's bighearted."

"I came about the pills in the hide-a-key box," he said. "You said Martin Hauptmann took one?"

"He took one."

"Right then? I mean while he was having his attack?"

"He was sagging to the pavement, clutching his chest."

"Did he look at them closely?"

She gave that a second to make sense. "He was in a lot of pain, Lieutenant. I saw him fumbling with the box. I don't suppose he examined them very carefully."

Skelote grunted. "Well," he said.

"Well what?"

"Well, that answers my question."

She didn't pursue it.

He started to turn, stopped. "Thanks," he said and kept standing there. "Hauptmann took baby aspirin. Not heart medicine. Baby aspirin."

"You think he got them mixed up?"

Skelote shrugged.

"Would you like to come in, Lieutenant?"

"Yeah," he said but didn't move.

The dead sausage got off the lawn and waddled to the trailer porch, as if sixth sense had it all over human communication any day. Nora Sandles followed it and Skelote fell in beside her.

"How long have you been separated?" she asked.

"The divorce was final two months ago."

She glanced at the faint mark that remained on his ring finger. "Maybe you do like dogs," she said.

They went inside where it was clean, neat, and bare-bones. Everything was plastic or vinyl; the cheap panels warped at the ceiling. The place had the unsteady hollowness of an empty ship on a sea of Jell-O.

"All right if I smoke?" he said, and it didn't sound like a question until she answered, "If you have to."

He plucked the cigarette out of his mouth and broke it in half. "I don't have to."

"My husband died of lung cancer."

"Oh."

The occluding silence led back to the dead sausage.

"I had a bulldog once," he said.

"Somehow I knew that."

"She was a great dog. I took her for walks all the time. A little wheezy, you know"—he tipped his hand back and forth—"but bulldogs are like that."

The bulldog had been a respiratory nightmare, and her top speed was a quarter mile an hour. He had come to the opinion that the breeding of something asthmatic and bowlegged, whose face could not contain its tongue, was cruel. In consequence he had tried to walk her to death as a form of euthanasia one balmy day. A long walk on a sandy beach. He would just keep walking, and eventually she wouldn't be there, he had thought. With her weak, runny eyes, she wouldn't be able to see him, her nose would be as effective as the inside of the eggplant it resembled, the sand would slow her bandy little legs to a still life, and when the tide finally came and went she would be buried at sea or far down the coast. But the uncanny beast hadn't gone to the bathroom in three days and left a trail like Hansel & Gretel bread crumbs, as if it had known it would have to find its way back. At least that was his interpretation. Long after sunset she had come wheezing up to the cottage they had rented. Skelote had made a guilty fuss over her.

"Bulldogs don't shed like collies," Nora Sandles said. "When we were kids we used to have 'fur fights.' "

The refrigerator cycled on like a Harley-Davidson.

"That your kids?" He pointed to a picture frame.

"Teddy on the left, Mark on the right." They were wearing sailor suits and sitting on their hands on the lid of a toy box. "It's twenty years old. Teddy works in Tampa; Mark is stationed at Fort Dix."

He started to tell her she didn't look that old, thought better of it. "I'm a grampa," he said.

"Would you like a beer, Grampa?"

"A beer sounds fine."

They got away from dogs and genealogies then, but not much closer to each other.

As Skelote was leaving, he glanced at the phone and memorized the number. He called her from the first pay booth, because that was more private than the station house.

"I forgot to ask if Hauptmann put his head between his knees after he took the pill," he said.

"I don't think so. No."

"Was he sitting down?"

"Yes."

"Was he breathing deeply?"

"I don't know."

"Could you tell if he just held the pill in his mouth rather than swallowed?"

"No."

"Would you like to see a show with me sometime?"

". . . yes."

■　　■　　■

NITROSTAT ANTIANGINAL. YOU were supposed to sit down, lower your head, breathe deeply. Don't swallow. The pill stayed under the tongue for five minutes. Hauptmann's doctor had said that. Skelote reached in his pocket and came out with a broken cigarette and the hide-a-key box. Maybe the box had held aspirin *and* nitro. He should have sent the whole thing instead of just the pill. The lab could pick up powder, do a trace. He got Catherton to run it over this time, wondering afterward why he had bothered. No matter what they said, there were still plenty of explanations. Quirks. He didn't need Hauptmann anymore. He had already met Nora Sandles.

When the report came back, it said aspirin. Again. But when Skelote asked specifically about Nitrostat, the chemist said it had to be kept in glass. Not metal boxes, not plastic. Glass. Martin Hauptmann was glass. Stained glass. Skelote looked through him and saw that the stain was red.

SIX

ANNA RECEIVED A brief acceptance note the week before Detlef
and Otto arrived unscheduled at the bus station in Padobar. She
took the call, then dispatched Ute in the family's old green Dodge
while she and Gerta hastened to make up the spare room downstairs. The mapping of authority between the two older women
was still incomplete. Anna was struggling to make it plain that
she could and would manage the studio; Gerta maintained a
watchdog attitude—clearly the studio was to her an extension of
the family, and Anna was not the head of the family.

"Did he say anything about the conditions in your letter?"
Gerta wanted to know.

"He just asked for directions and thanked me when I said I'd
send Ute."

"Did he sound . . . contrite?" Gerta pursed her lips thoughtfully. "He always sounded contrite when he wanted something, or
when he knew things were expected of him."

Anna fluffed pillows and didn't answer.

". . . but when he's arrogant, there's no controlling him," Gerta
finished soberly.

"I couldn't say whether he was contrite, or arrogant, or anything else, Mother. It was just a simple conversation. He was polite enough. And he's come. That should tell you something. My letter made it quite plain. I'm sure he understood. Anyway, he'll be here in a few minutes. You can judge for yourself then."

Gerta returned a stoical silence. If Anna wanted to run the studio, that was all right. Legally it was hers. But if she refused to keep it a family affair, how long would it take to fail? And what would happen to the family if they didn't all come together now and rebuild the spirit that had kept them unified since before the Goths had accepted Christianity?

"Anna," she remonstrated gently, "we are a couple of foolish women, you and I. You with your insecurity, I with my old woman's vanity. We want the same thing but pursue the method of getting it rather than the result. It will do no good to slaughter two chickens for the same pot. Let us share. Would I, Detlef's mother, confide my fears about him if I didn't have every confidence in you?"

"It was your suggestion to ask him in the first place," Anna replied somewhat more frankly, ceasing her preoccupation with the linen in the drawer. "You rejected my fears."

"And are you now punishing me for not listening to you?"

"It's too late now. He's here."

"But it's not too late to take a firm hold of things." Her vivid mahogany eyes, so curiously brisk in the withered face, widened energetically. "Anna, I believe that Detlef can be good for us—the studio. The eldest male Hauptmann, with two fine sons, can't you see that? They'll marry soon. The family will grow again and we'll see the craft prosper. Here! And yet he is Detlef. No illusions about that. I know my own flesh." She wagged her head. "A wild steed must be checked. You have to show him who's master. You, Anna.

That's why I'm concerned. Bridle him now. Take him aside and tell him immediately what you expect. No matter that you wrote it on a piece of paper and sent it to him. He said nothing about that in his reply, did he? Face him. Make him agree. It will only be harder later."

The sheet in Anna's hands snapped and canopied over the conversation. Gerta recognized the shroud.

The sound of the Dodge bottoming out on Chapel Lane announced Ute's return. Through the window they glimpsed the green hood winking among the firs, but it was impossible to discern the occupants. Flowing in tandem through the house, they arrived on the porch just as the car engine died. Kurt appeared in the doorway of the studio across the drive.

Detlef popped out first, like an old bull lunging into an arena. He nodded once to the women and swung around, fists buried in his pockets, eyes sweeping slowly from studio to chapel. He ended facing the car while Otto and Ute unloaded luggage.

"Do you see?" Gerta intoned to Anna.

Anna saw indeed.

Despair blanched her features. She didn't know what she had expected, but Detlef in the flesh appalled her. The old Detlef was there in his crooked stance, his scarecrow frame more tattered than ever, and in the jaunty flight of movement—elbow, knee, finger, head. She recognized his pauperistic charm in the looseness of his shrug and the elastic lean of his body as he nodded forward creating a smooth nadir from neck to heel. The mocking deadness in his eyes also struck a chord in her memory. But the blotchiness of his face, ruddy and pale, the gray-flecked hair, the bloated flesh coiled round his throat as if his jaw were eaten away, gave her a faint shock.

When the luggage was assembled, he strolled toward them,

swinging a suitcase against his thigh. The mocking deadness became radiance as he set the object down and immediately grasped Anna's two hands in his own cold grip. "How are you?" came out in a remnant of the voice she remembered. Then he bent to his mother's cheek.

"You look terrible," she declared.

"Time is cruel."

"Otto seems to have fared better, thank God." She beckoned forth a perfunctory kiss from her grandson. "Where is your brother?"

When there was no answer, she flashed Detlef a stricken look.

"Steeplejacking," he said bluntly.

Her cry silenced the birds in the orchard and brought Mackey and Jimmy Pelt to the studio doorway alongside Kurt. She reached out to them then. As a matriarch would. But the haunted look on Otto's face kept bringing her eyes back to Detlef.

▪ ▪ ▪

THE MEAL THEY ate late in the afternoon began very much like the one following Martin's funeral. Anna sat at the head of the table. Detlef filled out the balance of two to a side. The slow eating dragged until dusk, when Gerta got out the decanter of red wine from the elaborately carved *Kunstschrank* and poured six small glasses.

"To us!" she said, and they all felt relieved that it wasn't another toast to the dead.

Later, Anna took the flashlight and a set of keys and asked Detlef to accompany her to the studio. They crossed the drive, the light beam falling over the padlock on the door and trembling slightly in her hand as it narrowed. Once inside, she pushed the door to and snapped on the workbench lamp.

The old fluorescent tubes palpitated with energy, steadying one by one. Detlef's gaze rolled out to the faintly illuminated corners. With professional approval he noted the kilns, easels, light tables, propane torches, vises, glass cutters, grinding wheels, and—raising his head slightly to follow a scent—the renewing ether of kerosene and paint. He traced the sectioned bins of glass and the overhead racks of channeled lead cames and, above that, a ghosting gallery of sketches (called cartoons in the trade) on thick vellumlike paper.

But Anna hadn't brought him here to see the studio.

"You were probably outraged by some of the things I said in my letter," she began, "but they had to be said. And since you didn't give me any reassurances, I'm asking you point-blank: Do you understand about your drinking?"

With his chin still upraised to the cartoons, his eye fell upon her. "The drinking. Yes . . . I understand perfectly. You don't want me to drink to excess."

The exaggerated reverence as he folded his hands and dropped his chin disturbed her.

"And you intend to comply?"

"Oh, yes!" The words, whispered melodiously, seemed to vanish in the darkness above.

She should have stopped then, should have accepted the surface victory, but his arrogance kept her groping for dignity.

"I have nothing against you, Detlef. That should be obvious from the fact that you were invited to run the craft. And naturally I'm grief-stricken about Hans. But I've got my own crisis, and the studio is at a crossroads. We're not going to see that go down the drain now that we're starting to prosper. We can't let anyone stand in the way of that."

"We?"

"The family. You never used to think of me as family, I don't suppose that's changed. But I'm every bit a Hauptmann from craft to creed. Anyway, it doesn't matter, as long as you do your part. I don't intend to interfere unless things go wrong."

"Are those Martin's sketches?"

"No."

"Then you have a studio artist."

"Yes. Jimmy Pelt. If you're thinking of doing the cartoons yourself, or the glass detail, that's fine. But Jimmy stays. He and Bill Mackey have been loyal to us since we opened here. Neither will be let go under any circumstances."

"I really don't know if I can still draw," he mused as if she hadn't said anything else. "It's been years. But then, nothing is ever lost in this family, is it? I take it Otto and Kurt are to be trained."

"Yes. There's enough work. We've been in the process of expanding for some time." He nodded, pursed his lips. So much like Gerta, Anna thought. "Then we understand each other," she said. "There is to be nothing in your actions that will harm the studio."

She snapped off the workbench lamp, pausing in the darkness to hear his confirmation without the accompanying deception of a face. But she had made it a statement rather than a question, and the darkness was just darkness.

▪   ▪   ▪

IT WAS AFTER midnight when the real interview took place, the one in Detlef's room. Gerta broke the stifling silence with a hand hissing along the wallpaper as she came cautiously down the lower hall in the dark. She didn't bother to knock but pushed the door open so slowly that each syllable of its dry groan sounded like a separate rap.

He was sitting up in bed by that time, his face partly illuminated by the moonlight that fell full upon her. Eye to eye they met for a long while, and then she shuffled forward and eased onto a hard chair at the foot of the bed.

"Tell me about Hans," she whispered.

"Do you want me to resurrect him for you, Mother? He's dead. I carried his body myself, and I threw the first shovelful of dirt at the funeral. Don't ask me to remove it."

"He must have died almost to the hour when Martin did. Was it to drive us together in one place? Is it time for the family to reunite? Clearly the hand of God is in this."

"Or Satan's."

"Why are you so cruel?" She waited for perhaps thirty seconds, and then she asked in that marinated voice a little above a whisper, "Tell me about you, then."

"You can see what there is to know about me."

"I see where the shadow cleaves the light on your face. Tell me about your dark side. Do you still hate everyone for all your misfortunes?"

"One misfortune."

"Eva-Marie, yes, yes, we all lost Eva-Marie, but of course we weren't married to her. I loved her like a daughter, Otto never knew a mother, Eva-Marie lost her life—but it was *your* loss that mattered."

"No one else depended on her for what I did."

This was true. She had told Anna herself that love made the difference in a man like Detlef. Without Eva-Marie, he never would have smiled, as he had for a time.

"And you blamed Otto for her death," she said. "Otto who was the victim, not the cause."

"I raised Otto—"

"With anger and perhaps hate and not without vengeance!"

The darkness thrilled them both, because it came alive with his gathering passion. She felt it coming from the bed: the outpouring. And there was no longer any doubt in her mind that he was the one the family had been unconsciously waiting for.

"The craft is in danger of collapsing," she said.

"Anna says the studio is prospering."

"The craft, I said. You know what I mean. We're down to a precious few, and we're weak. It's a different world here, soulless. I'd like to believe that you've come to do the difficult things that must be done. That is your redemption, my son. If you have one, that must be your redemption."

She leaned away into a shadow, and when the moonlight found her again, she was shuffling toward the door. She looked back then. His face was still half-illuminated, but it was the dark side that seemed to contain the animacy.

Sometime before dawn Gerta got on her knees and thanked God for having sent Detlef to save the family, and for forgiveness because she had not understood years ago that Eva-Marie had been taken from them for this purpose. And she prayed for Hans's soul, while her ancient heart churned with misgivings, because she knew that Detlef's hate was still without direction.

SEVEN

BLACK CHRIST WANDERING in the swamp. Not forty days, but one night only. Detlef Brenemann Hauptmann.

Could it be me?

Anointed by his mother. Baptized by the death of his wife. Angel denied, so that he could live in everlasting pain.

Could it be me?

Hell is a cold place for some. Heaven a conflagration. For a time, Detlef had tried to live in between. For a time, he had walked the roofs of cathedrals, swung on the spires, hung from Gothic portals like a gargoyle. Now he had come down.

Could it be me?

He lacked the strength. Gravity had always sapped him. Age and dissipation were finishing the job. He was not afraid of dying; he was afraid of living. Because what if she was wrong? But she was always so sure, as if she had a direct pipeline to God. Damned and banished Detlef might not know, but could Gerta be deceived? And what made her think the enemies had come? Where were they? Always before they had come in self-righteous hordes, the heralds of kings, edict carriers of popes. The horrors of the past left no question marks. And yet in an oddly passive way he knew where the threat was. He had always known. It was implicit in his disdain for the faithless modern world, fallow with apathy. Was Gerta's Armageddon as insidious as that?

The chapel. That was where it must take place, if it took place at all. Right out in the open. Monstrously evident.

Martin was there when he arrived in the dark. He could feel him. Good Martin. Reluctant, to say the least. Enjoying death because it sanctified his miserably simple life. He had been a small man. A barely necessary link in the chain of the living family, producing in a lifetime nothing much more than what was produced before. But now he was dead, and therefore complete. If Detlef died now, he would have completed nothing. But, dear God, what was he supposed to produce? Silly geometries of glass that pleased gaggles of nuns? Torpid saints locked in two dimensions? Could he really be the one, the guardian at the gate? Why hadn't it come earlier then?

He pulled the door shut behind him and stood in the darkness for a few moments. Gradually the six faint shafts of light on the moon side of the chapel resolved themselves. Transversals from the high windows, like fallen beams across the nave.

The altar was a yawning abyss. No doubt, Martin was there. Slowly Detlef went to meet him. His steps were mortal detonations hurled back at him from the walls. When his boot toe struck the riser, he dropped to his knees.

"Touch me, Martin. If it's possible to reach across . . . touch me."

There was no draft to deceive him. No phantom silhouette. And he spread his fingers into empty space, groping.

"Martin? Hans? . . . Eva-Marie?"

And then he knew he was truly alone, truly separated from his own kind. God had him by the balls, and he began to tremble and to cry silently. He had not cried since he was a child, not even when Eva-Marie died. And then he did another childlike thing. He began to crawl. He crawled forward reaching out into the darkness, feeling febrilely like the damned and reviled things of an apocalypse. And when his hands rammed bluntly into the lectern, he scrabbled upward, fingers fluttering over the thin tissue facing of an open Bible. Immediately he tore off the page and backed slowly away.

He did not remember leaving the chapel, did not remember returning to the house or climbing the stairs or lying down on the bed. He might not even have closed his eyes. But when the light grew strong enough, he lifted the page. It was torn and creased, but he saw that it was from Romans, chapter nine, and he discerned two verses: "O man, who are you to reply against God? Will the thing formed say to him who formed it, 'Why have you made me like this?' . . . He has mercy on whom He wills, and whom He wills He hardens."

EIGHT

"GRANDMAMMA WILL KILL me, if she finds out!" Ute said.

"Oh, this is too funny for words." Otto kept looking at her sideways as they walked up Chapel Lane. "We really shouldn't waste it on a Stop 'n' Go."

Kurt stopped her, turned her. The foam throw pillow under her flannel shirt was slipping again. "Frau Hauptmann, as your obst . . . obst—as your baby doctor, I feel it is my duty to tell you that you are in labor. Would you like to give birth right here in the middle of the road or over there in the drainage canal?"

"*Obstetrician!*" she schooled him. "Are you sure you've done this sort of thing before, Herr Doctor?"

"In Germany I even delivered storks. Your baby's first words will be—what kind of sound does a stork make, Otto?"

"In German or in English?"

"How wonderful," said Ute, "my baby is going to be bilingual at birth."

"Actually, we suspect twins, frau. One German, one English." Kurt pushed the throw pillow up a little from the bottom, but stopped when his eyes met hers.

"You know, that's what's missing," Otto asserted.

"What?"

"Language. This baby should talk while it's still in the womb, or at least cry."

"Are you a ventriloquist?"

Otto waggled the microcassette player he was carrying. "You could slip this in there, Ute."

"Oh, really? What's going to hold it up? Never mind." She took the microcassette player, freed the top two buttons of the shirt, and tucked the device into her bra between her breasts. "So, how do I turn it on?"

Otto leered lustily. "Do you really want me to show you?"

"No, that would turn *you* on."

Kurt blushed as if she were speaking to him. He wished he had Otto's nerve with the opposite sex.

"I can just have it on when we go into the store," Ute said. "We'll leave a long blank at the beginning, then follow it with . . . what?"

"A dog barking," Otto said.

"No, not a dog."

"We'll all sing 'Brahm's Lullaby,' then."

"No one's going to be fooled by that. I thought we were going to make this seem real."

"What's real about a voice from the womb?"

"What about whistling?" Kurt suggested.

"Hey, that's a good one," Ute replied and plucked the microcassette out of her bra.

They stood in the dappled lane and recorded nonsense for the better part of an hour before settling on an airy, tuneless whistle that Ute managed to invest with innocence. Then, still laughing, they hiked to the Stop 'n' Go convenience store on the main road.

The boys went in first, pretending to be interested in magazines. Ute, her fingers splayed as if to support the small of her back, waddled in a scant minute later. Up and down the aisles she went, pausing near each of the several customers.

The first to look at her in astonishment was a short barrel of a woman with sunglasses on. She leaned to each side, peering behind Ute, and then the dark lenses fixed on the bulging flannel shirt. From the magazine rack, Otto and Kurt struggled for composure and wished they could hear what the woman with the sunglasses was saying.

The next person to be startled merely backed away with nervous uncertainty, while another stood stock-still, grinning. But it was the cashier who supplied the most entertaining response.

"Honey, I think something's happening to you," said the plump clerk with the heavy makeup. "I think you need to see a doctor right away."

"I feel fine," Ute said.

"No, really, trust me. I've had two kids. This is really strange."

"I'm okay," Ute assured her, cradling her pseudo pregnancy in both hands.

"When are you due, sweetheart?"

"Oh . . . any minute now."

The clerk sat up straighter, leaned forward. "Listen, I don't want to alarm you, but . . . something's wrong. Don't you hear anything?"

"No."

"Well . . . I mean, you've *got* to see a doctor, okay? Right away. I mean like right now. Okay?"

"I just came in for some Ding Dongs."

"Forget the Ding Dongs. Go see a doctor."

The boys were beside themselves, but Ute maintained character.

"I always eat Ding Dongs while I'm giving birth," she said.

"Oh, my God. This is *so* weird. Listen, are you sure you haven't . . . I mean, you can tell, can't you?"

"Tell what?"

"You just sit down, I'm going to call the fire department."

"I don't smell any smoke. But I've got to go now. How much for the Ding Dongs?"

"Keep the Ding Dongs! Just sit down."

"No, I'm going out in the parking lot and have my baby now."

She skipped to the door. "We'll help her!" Otto shouted, and he and Kurt dashed after her.

Outside, they all ran—gasping with laughter, turning back to see if they were pursued.

"What did she say, what did she say?" Kurt wanted to know about the first woman.

"She asked me if I had gas," Ute said with a gleeful sigh.

And they laughed again. Kurt and Ute and Otto on a magical afternoon of bonding near Padobar, Florida, in the fall of 1976.

They passed through the orchards and skirted the cypress swamp that touched the road there. And the greens were greener than normal and the birds flew rapidly and sang not a note, because something more than the usual afternoon baptism of rain was imminent. Even Otto seemed to sense this, though this was his first reconnaissance. He picked it up in Ute's eyes and in Kurt's silence. A breeze arrived like an exotic traveler, rushing out of the more impenetrable reaches of the swamp for all the world like a freight train, only with a ghostly sibilance that left them energized and struck by their own significance.

"We're invincible!" Ute affirmed the unstated premise.

And Kurt recalled his nervous fears en route from Germany. But he was half a Hauptmann already, wasn't he? The same blood—as much as Otto or Ute or Hans. The name Nehmer didn't change that. Why should the name matter? Or was there something else? Uncle Detlef still loomed darkly over his memory. There was something obscure there, something profane. It might be truly calamitous, or it might be the kind of childhood scar that stretches into adult disfigurement. But whatever happened, he was going to belong in this family. Whatever the fortunes of the studio, or the unpredictability of his uncle, nothing could change the pleasant foundations of a family. Nothing. Whatever the storm on the horizon . . .

■　■　■

BUT JUST OVER that horizon the sky coughed thunder.

A man named McIntosh heard it standing on his back porch with his cap and his pipe. He too knew that this would be no gentle benediction by amorphic clouds. The buoyant flocks of evening birds were grounded, and even the red-shouldered hawk, out for a final hunt, had trouble with the gusts.

Rasping his white whiskers, McIntosh entered the long narrow kitchen that sloped like a galley. He eased into the breakfast nook and stared out the window. A turkey buzzard had found some roadkill on the highway and was billing up elastic, blushing entrails as if they were sutures being tightened. McIntosh watched for a while, then went to the living room and turned on *Deadline News*. The weatherman was tossing chalk in the air and talking about Tacoma, Buffalo, Ashtabula. McIntosh fought to stay awake. Just before he nodded off, he saw the sweep of the radarscope revealing a line of heavy thunderstorms that had moved off the Gulf an hour before.

A *Hogan's Heroes* rerun was bumbling through the room when he awoke. For just a moment he had the eerie feeling of another presence in the house, and his eyes flicked to the mantel picture of his wife. He could have sworn he heard her checking windows the way she used to. Only she wasn't, of course. She had been dead eight years. It had to be the storm. Wind-driven rolls on the roof. A gust interrupting the gurgle of a downspout.

He fumbled for his pipe and tobacco. He filled the pipe, tamped the bowl, struck a match. It flared momentarily, neutralizing the blue glow of the match. But it went out before he could inhale.

Where was the draft coming from?

He stood quite still, taking quick, shallow breaths. Spasms of lightning left a residue in the room. The sky groaned. His eyes darted rigidly from shadow to shadow and suddenly shot to the bend of the breakfast nook. Something was crouching on the table . . . something was rising . . . expanding toward him, eyes scintillating out of the darkness. Three connected flashes exposed the onrushing mallet, but the sound never came. Because McIntosh was already dead by the time the smack reverberated through his brain.

The sky coughed thunder.

▪ ▪ ▪

"INVINCIBLE!" OTTO ECHOED against drumrolls of rain on the cypress that sheltered them, and an unknown deity or demon took a snapshot with a wink of lightning as if to preserve the irony.

NINE

So THEY HAD come together. Five Hauptmanns and a Nehmer.

For the first time since his father's death, Kurt felt the presence of a dominant male. And further back, his uncle recalled to him some child's perception deeply rooted in the past. In that past the grizzled face could no more be condemned than a favorite teddy bear's, its ragged hair suggesting movement (flouncing along with Otto on one hand, himself on the other—where?), the muzzy pockmarked brow as familiar as the macerated corner of some gray book that remained closed but compelling in his memory. Dimly he recognized that it must have been the pilgrimage to Chartres. Pilgrimage? The word echoed from childhood without definition. The experience of meeting his uncle and the motive for being sent at the age of six or so shimmered together and recrystallized as a series of half-formed images: Detlef framed against the window of a train; Detlef standing before the great cathedral; Detlef leading them through a shadowy place interspersed with novas of stained glass.

Gerta was less a mystery. Despite her age and accumulated wisdom, she seemed the most open and easily understood of the family. Her face fully committed itself to expressions as totally as a child's. Her eyebrows flickered like clipped wings. When they were up, they supported her face like clothespins; when they were down, she peered out of fleshy burrows and the stern dashes were scantily mimed by sparse hairs above a linear lip. He marveled that she didn't wear glasses, that she knew every bird in the compound by its song, that she knew to the moment when a pie was done without checking the oven. Her voice could cut the air with ratchety commands or summon forth purring sounds and gasps in a soothing blend children loved. He would listen endlessly to her talk about the old days, whether to describe the beautiful rose windows Martin had made in his youth or the spooky but harmless tales of forgotten ancestors who had suffered under the Inquisition.

And he saw that neither Ute nor Otto was immune to the charm of such tales. Listening was good for Otto's asthma, Anna would say. It made him forget to wheeze. Ute might perch on the very edge of the three-legged kitchen stool, looking like a fiery Valkyrie about to dive, or her lacquered nails might flash as she weaved a fan from egret feathers, her green eyes arranging the fine tracery as carefully as she arranged each item of food at meals. Already he knew there was something special about her. So methodical, so sure of herself. As if her life followed a script. She was in transit to some final outcome, and he wondered if she recognized that.

Kurt wanted desperately to belong here. And the obstacles seemed small and approachable. With Anna he had to overcome her preoccupation, emblemized by tapering blue ovals of cigarette smoke. With Otto the problem was a kind of reserve that lingered despite their foolishness in the Stop 'n' Go store. But that seemed to crack one day when he discovered a chameleon on the studio wall and pinned it by the tail only to have a full inch break off like clay beneath his finger. Astonished, Otto darted forward.

"How did he do that?"

"Don't know."

They looked at each other in wonder, and Kurt had the feeling that this bit of shared mystery connected them somehow apart from Ute. Together they learned the studio and corrected each other's English.

Ute took every opportunity to let them both know how badly they pronounced things. When Kurt made a reckless stab at French one day, she laughed in his face, informing him that he ought to keep peace with French, since he was already at war with English.

"A regular prodigy," Grandmamma assured them about Ute's linguistic ability. "At six months she spoke German like Goethe. It was all the alphabet soup Anna fed her."

There were other signs of patronage on Ute's part. She was a year older than Otto, two more than Kurt, and she liked to imply a secret fund of knowledge impossible for young boys to imagine. The mechanism for friendship exclusive of Otto, one clear blue morning, was cats.

She had just come round the Chapel Lane side of the compound to spoon cat food into the yellow plastic dish in the shed doorway; Kurt was there to move an old bench vise into the studio. She spooned while he wrenched at rusted bolts, and the two cats, tails periscoping, flowed elegantly between his shifting legs.

"They like you," she observed.

He bent to stroke the gray one.

Making a calipers of her thumb and forefinger, Ute pressed her temples theatrically. "You must be . . . a Gemini."

"Scorpio."

"Oh." Her face fell. "A spider. But you like cats?"

"Dogs, too."

He said it with gentle sarcasm, but she pretended not to notice.

"Uncle Detlef wants to get a pack of dogs. Hounds or something."

"Why?"

"To guard the compound at night, I guess."

"A pack of hounds? They'll have to be leashed. Why not a regular watchdog?"

He meant they would be off in every direction after nocturnal diversions, but she seemed to feel he had voted in favor of her cats.

"No big old dogs are going to chase you, Buttons," she cooed, gently rocking one of them. And rewarding Kurt with a warmer look than she had yet given him, she sashayed off bearing Buttons an inch away from puckered lips.

"*Angenehm*," he said to himself. *Agreeable.*

Thanksgiving was a benchmark in the progress of the studio. Anna, with the help of a pocket calculator, was gaining the upper hand on taxes, bills, and orders. They were getting sixty dollars a square foot for windows, she informed them as the turkey shrank slice by slice.

"We have much to be thankful for," Gerta concurred, nodding with approbation toward Detlef.

Later, tranquilized by dessert, the adults listened to Kurt and Ute washing dishes and arguing in the kitchen.

"You almost broke that glass!"

"I'm almost sorry."

"*Angenehm*," from Grandmamma as she rocked before the window.

▪   ▪   ▪

OUTSIDE THE FAMILY, it was Bill Mackey and Jimmy Pelt who eased Kurt's adjustment. Tender tutors. Mackey was the product of a sedate lifetime working glass; Jimmy Pelt bore the imprints of a broader world both literally and figuratively. There were the tattoos, for instance: a carmine rose stalked by a blue-black panther up one arm, the thrashing coils of a fanged cobra imperiling the shapely legs of a young lady, whose greater charms remained in Jimmy's rolled-up sleeve, on the other. And there was a scar that severed one coil of the snake. In humid weather it plainly caused the soft-spoken man a twinge of pain.

"Shrapnel," Bill Mackey explained one day. "That's his souvenir from the war. He doesn't want to forget."

And that was the kind of man Jimmy Pelt was, a man shaped and purified by experience.

It was Mackey who taught the boys about glass.

"What are these?" he would ask, tapping the slot in the glass bin that held round disks of rippled glass.

"Rondelles," Otto might answer.

"And this?"

"Cathedral glass . . . Marine antique," from Kurt.

"And this?"

"Slab glass." Kurt.

"Dalles." Otto clarifying. "Cut in thick slabs by a dalle-cutting hammer."

"And these?" Mackey would tip a box of random shapes in myriad colors.

"Jewels."

"Which side do you cut flashed stained glass on?"

"The unflashed side."

"And what . . . is this?" he might ask, withdrawing a sheet of the costliest variety, filled with random streaks and undulations, that they had seen Detlef himself fashion in the studio.

"Antique stained glass," from Kurt.

"Hand-wrought by a master," Mackey would augment. "Your uncle *is* that."

Somehow it sounded begrudging.

Then he had shown them how to handle glass, imparting an expert's knowledge: "You have to break the glass within a minute after you score it, otherwise the molecules will start to close ranks and you'll get an uneven break."

Like any artist, Mackey had an empathy for his medium. The glass was alive. It smiled or frowned; he read its expression by the light it transmitted. Often he would discard what looked to Kurt like a perfectly good piece, saying it was "sick." He never ceased caressing it with his eyes, and he executed cuts with surgical skill.

"You must *wound* the glass," he would say, dipping the cutter in kerosene before positioning a stroke.

In subsequent days Otto and Kurt were grozing edges and forming lead cames at his side.

What Mackey did for them in the lore of shaping glass, Jimmy Pelt equaled in decorating it. The gentle artist took them step by step through the sequence of making sketches, cartoons, preparing glass, painting details, and firing in the kilns. They became adept at the latter task through trial and error, firing projects at 1125 degrees Fahrenheit (cone 22 bends—a reference to fusing points) and even annealing a set of wind chimes. Kurt spent long hours watching the old man's tattooed hand stroke bold, stalwart portraits of the saints and in the process gained reverence for Jimmy Pelt.

There were other chores an apprentice learned. Taylor Jones, the young black boy who helped around the studio, taught Kurt to use low pile swathes of carpet for cutting. The resilience of carpet aided in the breaking, the pile absorbed fine slivers lost in the cutting. He also found him a pair of gray suede gloves to use when carrying panes. Taylor was fifteen, and the novel role of teaching something to older boys—white boys—was awkward for him. It was from Taylor that Kurt learned what the studio had been like before. A slower atmosphere, a lazy success, with "Mr. Martin" always preoccupied in puzzles of glass.

One misty Sunday just after Thanksgiving, Kurt was returning from the main road with the newspaper when he heard his name called. Turning, there was Taylor, breathless, the brown liquidity of his eyes vivid even through the mist.

"Accident . . . up the road!" he gasped. "Come on."

Kurt understood that it was the spectacle he was being invited to, not to render any kind of aid. It was excitement that made Taylor's eyes vivid. But there was still enough boy in him to answer that kind of imperative, and he gripped the newspaper and ran after Taylor without pause.

The road from Padobar funneled into a wall of cabbage and saw palmettos, Cherokee rose, trumpet vine, flame vine, hibiscus and camellia, looking stiff and coppery in the fog, which collected like webs over their faces as they ran. Abruptly there were pastures studded with rotten stumps, then a trailer park looming geometrically out of the morning. Taylor veered to the right, pointing. Kurt followed into a dirt lane that rose and was swaddled in gray banks. At some point beyond, a pulsing Merthiolate stain began to grow until it embered wide arcs of mist. Under it was an ambulance. The knot of figures standing quite still around the open bay doors was poor and black. Three vertical planes of successively weaker grays defined the rest: a small clapboard house streaked with orange and capped by a tin roof; a patched rail fence enclosing a small pasture flecked with odd bits of color; and finally the thick sinuous trees.

Near the fence a steaming roan tremoloed nervously, her saddle awry, one stirrup cut away. Two policemen were trying to calm her with low talk and slow strokes while the cone of pink light slipped glossily off her lathered flank. Now and then she reared, whinnied, and the whites of her eyes showed. She might have been distracted by the ambulance flasher, or she might have been unnerved by the smell of death freed from her stirrup.

Kurt got one glimpse of the body as it slid into the ambulance. A white body. Nearly naked. Shreds of clothes clotted with a bloody pulp of skin. The rest was dirt, raw muscle fiber, and huge contusions. A bone protruded outside the elbow, its beaklike head open and screaming. The roan, pulsing crimson with the flasher, drifted in his vision. Kurt stooped giddily to retrieve one of the flecks of color that dotted the ground. It was a scrap of plaid shirt, moist and smeared with viscera. Dropping it, he walked shakily to the road to wait for Taylor.

Ambulance doors slammed, an engine gently gunned.

"I never seen a dead man before," Taylor said.

His blackness was chalky in the mist, Kurt's whiteness nearly without outline, and their eyes met at the same latitude and longitude of growing up.

TEN

WHAT BOTHERED SKELOTE the most were the tracks. If the horse had shied, why hadn't it avoided circling over the spot where it had happened?

He knelt in the dirt, playing Indian. The way he read the prints, the roan had never deviated an inch from its path against the rail. Around and around it had gone until Adler looked like chili con carnage. Where Skelote thought he picked up continuity in the stride, it seemed like the animal had galloped. But then, the last time he had tracked a horse he was wearing a size eight Hopalong Cassidy suit and chasing a milk wagon in Beavers, PA.

He stood up, dusted his knees. Maybe the thing it had shied from was in the center of the little pasture. Maybe that was what had kept it in a panic. Maybe.

He took a stroll.

The brown grass was chewed short for the most part but sewn too tight for marks. There was no snake, no flash of color, no wadding from an exploded firecracker. And no sense trying to understand horse sense.

He switched to Adler's motives. The man had lived alone in a clapboard shack with a tin roof, and he had gotten out of bed one morning before you could see your hand in front of your face and jumped on his horse and galloped around like they were training on a carousel for the Derby. It was a very odd thing to do. Even a recluse living alone, who had maybe gotten out of sync with the rest of the world, wouldn't normally get out of bed for R and R before the mist was off the ground. Unless it was to ride a night mare.

He got back in his Plymouth, drove the fifty yards to the next house, got out, knocked on the front door. He could see the occupants ghosting behind the curtain, watching him watching them. They had probably been out there when the prime cut was on display, but now they weren't even going to answer the door.

The one who finally came had cold sores and stringy hair that might have belonged to an auto mechanic specializing in oil changes, except that if you looked close you could still see it was a woman.

"Police, ma'am." He played out the flap on his wallet and whizzed it shut again with the same gesture. "I'd like to ask you a few routine questions about your neighbor." She kept studying him like he hadn't said anything, and he added, "Mr. Adler."

"Is he dead?"

"Yes. Did you see anything this morning?"

"An ambulance."

"Did you hear anything?"

"It didn't have no siren."

"Did you see or hear anything before the ambulance?"

"No."

"Did Mr. Adler ride horses a lot?"

"Every damn morning."

"Before dawn? Even in a mist?"

"Even in the rain. In the moonlight sometimes. Crazy old coot."

"Did anyone ever visit him?"

"Adler?" She laughed ponderously. "He don't even get junk mail. Didn't, I mean."

"Did he have any enemies? Any problems in the neighborhood?"

"You think he was murdered?" She began winding a strand of stringy hair around her finger, like a little girl. "Well, I don't know who would bother. He threw a rock at a Jehovah's Witness once. Maybe God done him in."

"Is there anyone else at home here?"

"Ed."

"I'd like to speak to Ed, too."

"That's him right there in his wheelchair."

She stepped aside, and Skelote peered past. Ed had chrome spokes.

"Hello, sir," Skelote said, taking a step into the room.

"Ed's deaf," the woman said.

Skelote left her with a religious look on her face and her finger wound up in a polyester rope.

The rest of the neighborhood felt about the same. Adler was the man who didn't answer the door on Halloween, seldom spoke, and rode a horse around his postage-stamp pasture as if it were the perimeter of the earth. Judging by the contents of his three-room shack, he wasn't even conversant with the walls. Skelote went in twice to look. There was nothing to indicate he had ever really settled in. No pictures, no curtains, no shelves or hooks or a nail to hang a fly swatter on.

No fly swatter.

There was indoor plumbing, toilet paper, soap, a razor, a re-

frigerator that kept a jar of salad dressing and some garden veg-
etables at fifty degrees or so, a closet pole wedged across a corner,
some junkyard furniture, and a well-thumbed Gideon Bible. The
closet pole had two changes of clothes slung over it. There wasn't
even a mirror. Adler must have shaved looking at his reflection in
a pan of water. Could living alone do that to a man? No wonder
he had jumped on his horse every morning. The place was full of
emptiness.

It made Skelote feel at home. He was glad there wasn't a mirror here. He didn't want to see himself.

But right after breakfast he called Nora Sandles and invited
her to a show. They saw *Return of the Pink Panther* that night, and
afterward they drove to an Italian restaurant in Cicadia. Then they
took another drive. Then they parked near the tennis courts in
Padobar and walked around the duck pond. Skelote dreaded making a move, dreaded not making one. A Muscovy duck hissed
faintly in the dark.

"How about a Dairy Queen?" he asked Nora Sandles. He
couldn't see her face, but he sensed radiance and relief.

They got Dairy Queens, and he ducked into the bathroom to
smoke a cigarette. He had smoked one in the Italian restaurant
and was sure she hadn't known. He did it the same way this time,
blowing smoke in the toilet bowl to keep it off him, chewing up
three Certs, spraying his coat lightly with something that had
retsin in it, and washing his hands.

"Look, don't smoke in the john," she said when he came out.
"Forget what I said the other day about my husband dying of lung
cancer. Just do it in front of me. Okay? I mean that. Light up right
now. Here. Where do you keep your cigarettes?" She patted him
down, pulling the pack and a book of matches out of his inside
pocket. "Now. I want you to do what you want. I know you can't

help it." She poked a cigarette in his mouth and lit it somewhere near his lips.

Skelote coughed. He felt like a gorilla with its face on fire.

"There. How's that?" She ended up swatting him on the back, and the cigarette fell to the ground.

"I really didn't need another one," he muttered.

"Oh, God. What's the matter with me? Maybe you want to call it a night."

Skelote thought about Marcus Adler's empty shack. "Not unless you do."

She broke into a smile and then a laugh. "My, my, a glutton for punishment. You've certainly been a gentleman. Well, my place or yours?"

He looked stunned. "How about a walk?"

"We just took one. Are you in training or something? Oh. It's too soon after your divorce, is that it? Now I'm being insensitive."

He scoffed that one off unconvincingly, and they walked and all he could talk about was Adler's death.

"I make too much of these things sometimes," he said. "It's the frustrated cop in me. Last month it was Martin Hauptmann's heart attack. Hell, the closest I've been to a murder in a couple of years is that bludgeoning way over in Palm Hollow. Still, I can't figure Adler. I mean, okay, live alone long enough and you get a zip code for the moon, but riding a horse around and around in the middle of the night practically, what's that, a cure for insomnia?"

And when he realized she was reading Jack Skelote's autobiography in the emphasis on loneliness, he switched to unknowable aspects of Adler's life. How had the old man come by a horse in such poverty? How had he gotten a saddle? Did the horse live on just grass and water?

The more he talked, the safer the distance between him and

Nora Sandles seemed to get, and he said good night at her trailer feeling he had struck a balance he could live with. And Marcus Adler, too, seemed to have served his purpose and been laid to rest.

Accident.

Case closed.

ELEVEN

"OF COURSE THEY'RE just hounds!"

Detlef spoke much too loudly for the dinner table. And that was curious to the rest of the family, because they all remembered the liquor-locked whisper with which he had arrived from Germany. The cough was still there, nagging and convulsive, but the voice was unbridling itself.

"They're the strangest-looking hounds I've ever seen," Anna remarked with a languor meant to lead Detlef down a few decibels.

"More like wolves," said Ute, flashing green fire at her uncle.

"Wolves?" Detlef was in his "High German" state, as Gerta called it, an animated fever of talk that came out the same in English as in his native tongue. "They're the very nemesis of wolves. They were bred in carnal hate of wolves—"

"I thought you said you didn't know the exact breed," said Anna.

"The breed is immaterial. They aren't purebreds. No purebred could do what they can do. But even an untrained eye can see the Irish wolfhound in them. Big dogs . . . massive. The brindle must weigh as much as Kurt. And they have borzoi blood!"

"What is it that they *do?*" Anna interjected dryly.

"Do? They have jaws powerful enough to bring down a wolf. The old borzoi would course their prey until they got him—right here." He touched his throat below the ear. "One on each side. A wolf is strong enough to toss a sheep with his neck, but not a hound such as these—"

"I hope they're long-winded," said Anna, "because the nearest wolf short of Busch Gardens is apt to be in Canada."

Detlef blinked. "They'll make good watchdogs."

A round of barking from the compound brought them all to the reality of the black and brindled pack he had purchased that morning, three animals chained outside the chapel. No one could remember hearing barks so compelling and savage.

"They're vicious!" Ute rankled.

"Only to their enemies. By nature they're very tractable toward people. In fact I will have to train them to be watchdogs."

"How are they toward cats?"

"I assume your cats can climb trees? Anyway, they will be chained."

There was a long frustrated silence.

"How is your painting," Anna asked then, "returning to form?"

He glanced at his fingers smudged with pigments, held the hand high. "It never left. Like driving a car."

"Has anyone heard when Marcus Adler's funeral is to be?" asked Gerta.

"Wednesday," Kurt said.

"Poor old Marcus. Harmless and God-fearing. We could all see that. Even without second sight, we could all see that."

Kurt looked uncomfortable. Second sight was another little family trait he seemed to lack.

"Why was Marcus out riding so early in the morning?" Anna wondered aloud. "They say it was foggy."

"He was . . . eccentric," Gerta reflected in measured tones.

From the chapel came a discord of snarls. Detlef's fork clattered to the plate.

"Impatient to be mastered," he said, tossing his napkin down. In a moment the screen door slapped shut behind him.

"Mamma, how could you let him!" Ute unleashed tearfully.

"There's plenty of room in the compound, Ute, and as long as they're chained . . ." Anna extracted a cigarette from the pack by her plate.

"But you promised!"

"I said I'd think about it. I have. Detlef is in charge of the studio, and he thinks it's important to have watchdogs."

"Important for what? Nobody's going to steal from us."

"Stained glass is not without value."

"Grandmamma . . ." Ute began in a final, reckless appeal. It was side-taking in the power struggle between Anna and Gerta, an acknowledgment of where true authority lay, but she could not stop. "Grandmamma, tell her. We don't need dogs. Uncle Detlef has no right!"

"If it's the studio, he has every right, child."

If. Everyone understood the circumvention of that answer, and no one dared explore it. Even outspoken Ute knew she had reached the limit of leeway.

Anna brought the cigarette to her lips in long quiet draws. Kurt chewed. Otto spooned a final crescent of Jell-O from the side of his saucer. And then, as if by consensus, the teens rose one after the other to leave. When they were gone, the two women sat at opposite ends of the table. Gerta spoke first.

"Did he ask before he bought them this morning?"

"No," replied Anna, blowing a thin jet of smoke through each nostril. "No, he did not."

▪   ▪   ▪

THE DOGS CHORUSED wildly as Detlef came through the pines, flexing his fingers into a pair of leather gloves. Two blacks and a brindle. Huge dogs. Deep chests, retracted loins. They were harnessed on three traces to the iron handle of the chapel door, and true to their Russian blood, they strained as though they were pulling a troika.

He went around the far side, unlocked the cellar, descended the twelve steps, felt for the light. The place smelled of paint and thinner and fresh cut pine bleeding gummily in the dampness. Sawhorses, benches, and rusted tools cluttered one half; on the near side yellow sawdust clung in colonies to moist patches over the cracked stone. Against that wall, beneath where the stopcocks for propane gas jutted, stood three newly hewn crates.

He opened the reinforced door of the first, collected a heavy sisal rope and the handled end of an oak oar he had sawn in two, and ascended the steps. Leaving the cellar door ajar, he tucked the half oar under his arm and began to fashion a sliding noose.

"Cerberus," he called playfully to the three of them.

Then he swung the noose over the brindle, unsnapped his collar, and jerked him up taut.

Surprised, the big animal wheezed and pawed. He had never known abuse. The human had made a mistake and would presently loose him. But the prodding tip of the oar goaded him toward the cellar. He danced sideways, snapping savagely, and the rope whipped taut again, searing his throat. He stiffened. Then bracing his four paws, he worked his jaws, bringing forth a belated cough. The weaving club flashed to his flank, and this time he sprang at the man. Again the rope jerked him off course, and a stunning blow to the side of his massive head left him lolling bloodily in the dirt.

"Is that all from you?" said a patient voice.

The brindle tried to paw himself along, growling a single sustained note like a record caught in a groove. As the hot humming pain cleared, he lunged at the man yet again. And now the club crashed on the side of his neck. Down he went, tongue out, black lips flecked, gurgling.

"That's the spirit."

Then the sole of a boot launched him down the cellar steps, flailing wildly. At the bottom, his nails hissed briefly over stone. The next moments were dim to the animal—rough movement, cold, darkness. Then the water. A thick stream of it, icing him into a frenzy. The rope was gone. He sprang upward, colliding with the sides of a crate, water sluicing all around. And when at last the human—the enemy human—made the water stop, the brindled creature had gotten in touch with all its ancestral traits: the cunning, the aggression, the hate, the will, and especially the fierceness of the wolf.

■   ■   ■

KURT STEPPED OUT of the shed in the twilight, sanding the edge of a rondelle. Ute stood on the little flagstone walk overrun with catbrier searching the shadows of the shed and the orchard for fluid silhouettes. Overhead a cruciform cluster of bright pinpoints crawled toward a distant airport, trailing sound like jettisoned cargo.

"They won't come now," he said. "It's not their dinnertime."

She threw him a resentful look and banged the plastic dinner dish like a tambourine.

Kurt displayed the circle of glass, faintly rubescent in the gathering night. "I messed up three of these today," he said.

"They're gone for good," she said about her cats.

"They'll be back, Ute."

"They won't ever come back." She looked quite certain.

"Oh. I forgot. You've got second sight."

Her eyes swept the orchard again and came to rest on him. "What do you mean by that?"

"I don't know what the hell it means. That's the point."

"You make it sound like it's important?"

"If it's not important, why is it such a big family secret?"

She laughed one syllable. "Momma said you were insecure."

"Your mother said that?"

"Actually, your mother said it to mine."

"My mother would never say that."

"Yes. She did. She wrote it in her letter. And look how insecure you are over that."

"Oh, sure. Like I shouldn't be."

"Why does it matter, if it isn't true? And if it is true . . . well, you should have the courage to recognize it."

"Thank you, Ute Margit, for your blueprint for living. By the way, my sister, Monika, said you were stuck up."

"Really?" she replied airily.

"Really."

They looked at each other for one tongue-tied moment, and then the facades cracked into wry smiles.

"I can't believe we're cousins," Ute said in an undertone. "You're so shy and polite, and I'm stubborn and opinionated. Feel free to contradict me."

Kurt shrugged. "I'm not opinionated, how would I know?"

"Maybe you're not so polite either. Do you like the Beatles?"

"George and John are pretty cool."

"I like Paul."

"Figures."

"Why?"

"I don't know."

"You wanta hear some tapes?"

"Sure. When I'm done at the studio."

"Come get me afterward. I'll be helping Mamma with the accounts." She turned away, spun back. "And second sight is nothing to get hung up over. It's just an intuition really. Grandmamma says it kept the family alive through the Inquisition when telling the God-fearing from the profane sometimes meant getting clear of the church's wrath."

"I must be missing some special gene."

"When you go through second confirmation you'll probably find yourself. Not to worry, cousin."

Second sight . . . second confirmation, that awakened something. His sister had gone through a second confirmation at the age of ten or eleven. That was when he had been away at Chartres with Uncle Detlef. When he returned after a week, she seemed different. His mother said she had been transformed by the experience, that she knew the family history back to the beginning now. Who had told her, he wanted to know. No one had told her, his mother had answered. She remembered. Remembered? And when he turned twelve and asked about his second confirmation, he was told he wasn't ready yet. How did you get ready? You grew old enough to understand, he had been told. You demonstrated second sight. And when it was strong enough, you fasted. His sister had fasted for days before he left on his journey with Otto and Uncle Detlef. She was weak and heady when he left, in no condition for much of anything, he reflected now. Is that how it was triggered—by breaking down resistance and rationality? Transformed, indeed. He had almost forgotten that. He searched his mind for an association with what had happened at Chartres.

Ute went back to thumping her tambourine. Kurt looked to the chapel tower pointing at the icy glitter of stars, and below that—far, far below—the full-throated rumble of enraged hounds seemed to be answering her.

TWELVE

THE PHOSPHATE PLANT outside Padobar looked like an abandoned city melting into the plain. Chalky turrets and loading elevators gave it a profile, but even at full operation the vastness of its excavations dwarfed its vitality. At twilight, a network of widely spaced lights blinked on bank by bank, and the sectors came to resemble empty Christmas tree lots.

Steve Laberdie liked that look. Usually he ran the perimeter in one of the plant security's electric carts, feeling its magnitude and gazing childlike at the warm suffusion of so much orange light. At forty-four he had worked plant security for sixteen years.

Just after nine P.M. on the night Skelote was eating ice cream with Nora Sandles, he made his run to the north end equipment depot. Out across the paved parking lots, over the old road to where they were building the new one, he drove the whining cart, enjoying the fact that it was his noise, his dust, his movement that dominated the huge complex. There were nights when those same things could intimidate you, when you felt too obvious and vulnerable in the presence of something larger. But not tonight. Tonight there was no larger presence.

The north end depot held mostly road-building equipment now. A glance through the chain link showed more order than usual. Someone had taken the trouble to park the grader so that it wasn't blocking everything, and the diamond saw for sectioning pavement had its protective shield in place. That was why he was surprised to see the yellow hard hat lying on the brink of the trench outside the fence.

Either they put things away or they didn't. Usually. But this time the gate was locked and the stuff all arranged, except for that one bright yellow hard hat as plain as a blimp in a ballroom.

Sorting through the keys on his belt caddy, he climbed off the electric cart and walked over to the edge of the ditch. "Son of a bitch," he said to himself when he stooped to pick up the hat. Because there was another one in the trench.

That burned him. Two of them. A couple of malcontents just hadn't cared. Kids were always coming through the construction area, grabbing up what they could. That cost the company money and in the long run hurt the workers. Anyway, whenever anyone noticed something missing, they blamed plant security. That hurt Steve Laberdie.

At one end of the nine-foot-deep ditch was a run of wooden ladder. The hat was at the other end. Laberdie backed down the wooden steps, trudged the length of the trench, and stooped again. But before he could pick it up, he heard a faint lisping noise that froze him in the act of grasping. He glanced backward. *The ladder he had just descended was gone.*

And now he felt it. The larger presence. Coming from above him, above the edge of the ditch. He never did pick up the hat. Because looming there, out of the corner of his eye as he cocked his head, was a human silhouette. Its legs were braced, its arms raised above its head, its hands linked by another silhouette, a rough uneven silhouette.

Like a piece of jagged concrete.

Steve Laberdie dove away from the first one as it came hurtling down, and it hit the soft earth with a thud, deceptively soft, like distant shore batteries once had made in Korea. He had survived then.

He spat the dirt from his mouth and was scrambling for the end when the second chunk of concrete cut him off. This one brushed his scalp, and he thought it had opened a wound, but it was just the raw coolness of a grazing miss.

The third missile caught his shoulder, radiating pain through half his body. That half of him went dead, and he rolled onto his back, squinting helplessly at the macabre silhouette performing its simian ballet against a mauve sky. Again and again and again. Until the other half of him went dead.

THIRTEEN

SKELOTE PUFFED BLUE smoke all over his living room as if dusting for clues. He had rented the little flat after the divorce from Claudia. It was too small, too expensive, and too close to the cattle shed of a neighboring farm, but it was a soft place to land after Claudia. Soft furniture, soft wallpaper, soft lighting, soft carpet.

Nora Sandles invited you in, dummy, he thought. *And you didn't go. You left her at the door.*

The blue smoke sank into the carpet. Skelote exhaled a fresh batch.

Okay, you were supposed to feel guilty after a divorce. Sometimes you even felt unfaithful when you moved on, even though you knew you were free, even though infidelity had never made you feel guilty while you were married. He thought about that lone episode on the way to the station. It had taken place sometime after Claudia had cut their sex life down to celibacy. The object of his passion was Ida "the hop" Fogel, Padobar's patron saint of stray cats and only tenured whore. In general, she did the town a service by keeping all its strays off the streets. A few bachelors, a few degenerates, one or two discreet husbands with unappeasable fetishes, now and then an adventurous high school student who couldn't score in his peer group, Ida "the hop" relieved them all.

When business dropped, she occasionally went street-walking in the evening at the main intersection, which was a short block from the Baptist church, and inevitably there would be a complaint. It was on one of these occasions that Skelote himself had ordered her into the backseat of the patrol car, partly because he happened to spot her first, partly because he was horny and frustrated and it didn't seem right to him that anyone else should have sex when he was horny and frustrated. She had been walking around in a red mini that didn't quite cover her garters, and she had held a white kitten to her face like it was a compress. He had it in mind that he would just drive her out of town with a lecture and let her go at the truck stop a few miles away. But she must have sensed his vulnerability on this particular night, because she had extended the kitten to him and said: "You want a little pussy, Lieutenant?"

He had decided he did, and they turned up a dirt road alongside an orange grove. It was pretty dark by that time, and Skelote had thought he could go through with it if he didn't look at her too long. They had gotten situated on a patch of grass before he began to change his mind. He had seen cleaner wheel bearings, he decided. But he was angry at Claudia. She had it coming to her. She was supposed to be his wife, and she had it coming. So he did it with Ida "the hop."

He punched on the two-way radio now and drove slowly in the morning traffic. Two blocks from the station, the static keyed up a little and a voice broke through, advising that there was an ambulance run to the Norris phosphate plant south of town. He heard Catherton take it and code back a 10-51, which meant en route. Skelote was about to cancel him—the phosphate plant should be handled by the sheriff's patrol, since it was mostly outside township limits—but what the hell, the station wasn't air-conditioned and his car was.

He got through another cigarette before Catherton's flasher came in sight. The ambulance was returning to the plant gate already, moving like a hearse. Even driving slowly, Skelote buried it in a cloud of dust. A huge gravel mound caught the passes of the cruiser flasher, and Catherton himself was ankle deep two yards up the slope. He had his fingers wrapped around a bottle of Old Grand-Dad, whose label Skelote could read from the car.

At a discreet distance around the base stood a mixed group of laborers and shirt-sleeved managerial types, craning as if they were in Lady Godiva's dismounting area. Skelote crunched up the two yards of gravel in eight steps.

"I was just trying to figure out how much gravel it would take," Catherton said, hefting the bottle.

"To redo your driveway?"

"I've got asphalt, sir."

"Don't tell me what happened, Catherton, I can't stand straight answers when I'm totally in the dark."

"The plant security man was killed in a gravel slide." He gestured from where the apron of gravel extended in a twenty-foot crescent at the base to the unstable cleft near the top of the mound. "Nobody saw it, but I figure he was up there drinking this."

Skelote squinted at the top, thirty feet high more or less. "He was buried at the bottom?"

"With just his hand sticking out. Some construction workers saw his electric cart and found him."

"Where exactly did you find the bottle?"

"At the bottom. It must have slid down with him."

Skelote took the thing. It was barely scratched.

A dumpy man in a soiled dress shirt and loosely knotted green tie lumbered onto the scene then. Despite his oddly petite pace, he was breathless and flushed.

"Are you in charge, Captain?" he mistakenly identified Skelote. "I'm Dexter Logan, assistant supervisor of operations. Consider me at your service for any questions. I was one of the first to come on the scene. We've got a good safety record here, and we want to get to the bottom of this. But you see the bottle, Captain. It's pretty clear what happened, isn't it? I suppose Laberdie went up there to do a little drinking on the job, and the pile just came down."

"Laberdie?"

"Steven Laberdie."

"How long had he worked here?"

"A dozen years, maybe fifteen."

"Did he have a drinking problem, Mr. Logan?"

"I'd have to check his file." Logan mopped his neck.

The company was scared to death of OSHA. Logan had to decide what the company position would be, whether they knew of any drinking or not.

"Can we see that file now?" Skelote asked.

Logan puckered, nodded. "Yes, I suppose we can go check personnel."

The personnel division was two filing cabinets and a dusty secretary. The fine powder that hung in the air had gotten into everyone's pores. Skelote thought he could understand why an employee might climb atop a gravel mound to wet his whistle. He might have wanted a panoramic view to go with the mood, or he might have wanted a clear view of anyone coming to check up on him, or he might have been clawing for air at the top of this dust bowl.

The file disagreed. Laberdie had an unblemished record. No alcohol, no goldbricking. Five days sick leave in the last two years. Once he had earned a bonus for a suggestion. His current evaluation said "loyal and conscientious."

"He certainly was discreet about his drinking," Logan said. "But then we're very safety conscious. Laberdie would have known that." He seemed relieved. There was nothing in the file a sharp Miami lawyer could grasp, accusing them of contributory negligence for not insisting Laberdie be treated or for turning him loose in the complex knowing he was a danger to himself.

Skelote left Catherton to wrap it up and went back to Padobar and the phone calls that defined his days. At two o'clock he called the medical examiner's to get a report on the body. They had never heard of Steven Laberdie. Miffed, he called Palm Hollow Emergency to find out why they were sitting on a stiff.

"The body was released four hours ago," said the duty nurse.

"Who'd you release it to, the butcher?"

"Kryzel-Tomlinson funeral home. Properly authorized."

The next call brought up a voice marinated in the hereafter. "We took charge of the deceased this morning, Lieutenant."

"Cancel cosmetics. I don't want a lawn over that body yet."

The voice from the hereafter drifted away, replaced by one that had a business abruptness: "Kryzel."

"Lieutenant Skelote, Padobar Police, Kryzel. You've got a customer name of Steven Laberdie, routed wrong. Now, I know you don't get much repeat business, but when the examiner is through you can have this one back."

"Better check with Chief Wagner, Lieutenant."

"I run this department, Kryzel. Harry Wagner is a political appointee and he keeps his nose out of my office."

"Check with him anyway, Lieutenant."

Kryzel hung up.

The next call went to Chief Wagner's wife's real estate office. "Since when do you one-up me, Harry? Since when do you run the station out of that land operation?"

"An old friend came to me, Jack," Wagner said softly. "Steven Laberdie's brother. The family is embarrassed. They don't want to read that he died while drinking on the job. An autopsy won't be necessary."

"What if Laberdie wasn't drinking?"

"Gravel piles don't make good murder weapons. Don't you think the family would want justice if they thought he was murdered?"

"The family could be wrong. They could even be implicated. Did you ask them if Laberdie drank heavily?"

"I didn't have to. He did."

"They told you that?"

"I knew him. He did."

"Don't expect me to lie to reporters who come asking questions, Harry. I've got suspicions."

He had no suspicions. Laberdie's death was accidental. But an autopsy was required in Marlo County, and he didn't like having the law rearranged over his head. It was politics, it was pride. That was why he decided to raise a little hell by calling the phosphate plant to advise Dexter Logan that no autopsy would be performed.

"We've already reached a tentative settlement with the family," Logan informed him.

Ah. The whole cake. The family wouldn't hold up the company; the company wouldn't make the circumstances public. Old refrain.

The next call he made was to Nora Sandles.

FOURTEEN

"I don't think they'll ever get back together again."

They were eating lunch in the orchard the week before Christmas and Otto's lament was about the Beatles. Kurt, lying on the grass with his cap covering his eyes, took a cue from Otto's words and softly sang the lead line of "Get Back."

"Of course they'll get back together," Ute said, her long white fingers playing the tape recorder's buttons like a trill as she rewound and restarted "Hey, Jude."

Kurt came up on one elbow. "Maybe they're just waiting for the Maharishi to bring their manager back from the dead."

"They said Paul McCartney was dead, too," Otto observed.

Kurt flopped back on the grass, his arms flung over his head. "And they were right," he sneered.

"Blasphemy!" Ute cried, straddling him in an instant and pinning his forearms under her weight. "Take it back."

Kurt was shocked. The feel of her animated weight and the accommodation of her hips electrified him. But the context was challenge rather than sex, and outwardly he reacted in kind. "Never," he spluttered.

"Admit Paul is the best! Say it, Paul is . . ."

"A dinosaur rocker." He struggled, but she was too strong.

"Say it."

"You're crazy. Like that nurse in the movie last night." They had gone to see *One Flew Over the Cuckoo's Nest,* which had finally reached Padobar after winning five Academy Awards.

"Nurse Ratched," Otto supplied.

Kurt wriggled one wrist free, and Ute sprang to her feet. She had a good thirty feet head start by the time he scrambled up. The breathless chase spiraled through the orchard, knocking oranges from low-slung branches, growing weaker and slower. It ended with Mackey's call from the studio, signaling that it was time for the boys to get back to work; and Ute, now halfway to the house, turned to render a mocking, gasping reprise of "Get Back" for their return.

"I took a piece of your puzzle!" Kurt hollered from the orchard, referring to the one-thousand-piece jigsaw landscape she was building in the house. "I'm going to erase 'Hey, Jude'!"

But all he got was lyrical laughter.

"Did you really take a piece of her puzzle?" Otto wanted to know as they walked back to the studio.

"No, but I'm going to. She has to get it off the dining-room table before Christmas dinner anyway."

Resuming the day's tasks, they found Mackey mildly perturbed at the new order of things. "I'd like to make a pattern, if Herr Hauptmann would approve," he said. "You don't s'pose he's up there in the chapel? I hear the dogs rumblin'."

The question seemed to fall to Otto. Reluctantly, the young immigrant put down the lead came he was forming and wiped his hands on the back of his pants. Kurt could see how he dreaded going. Whatever had happened on that roof in Germany was still happening in Otto's mind, and the passing weeks had clearly revealed the rift between father and son.

"I'll go," he offered, tossing his suede gloves on the workbench. Otto nodded once in gratitude.

The long fine needles of the pines seemed to mist the light around the chapel, so that no matter how sunny the day there was always a haze there. Kurt was surprised as he squinted through this to see that one of the stained-glass windows was covered with a weather-beaten shutter. Ruby tints dripped through the slats against the light from the eastern face. A ladder lay partly exposed behind the building. The front door was locked.

He circled to the cellar annex and found it open. The smell should have warned him. But he had come on a routine task, and his mind was elsewhere. Hand outstretched to the moist wall, he descended one slow step at a time, and at the bottom, just before the low growl came to him, he captured a single quick impression: scintillating eyes behind slats in crates, a jumble of stored things, a drizzling hose feeding the drain—

"What the hell are you doing here?" Detlef roared, rearing out of the shadows suddenly.

What happened next was almost a reflex. Before Kurt could utter a word, his uncle brought the flat of his hand across his face. It was a useless blow. Kurt made a willowy bend, returning to plumb as straight as a soldier, but the surprise was profound. Detlef, too, seemed surprised, though he raised his malletlike hand again. It came so slowly this time that it was almost a warning. Kurt sprang up the steps away from the whole melee of barks and curses, throwing the cellar door shut and running, running, not even glancing back until he reached the pines.

And it was in this attitude that Gerta saw him as she carried a small green pail of oranges toward the house. The great sinkholes of her eyes calmly absorbed his crisis. She waited while he tried to keep on walking, pretending all was well.

He knew he wasn't fooling her, and as if reaching the end of a tether he faltered and turned. From twenty feet, her gaze seared over him like a heat lamp. Knuckling the blood back toward his lip, he hung his head.

"He won't touch you again," she promised grimly. "Wash in the shed and go back to the studio."

He was no good at acting. If he went back to the studio now, they would all know what had happened. He couldn't stand the thought that the newly gelling family relations might come unglued. Detlef was the cotter pin. Without a studio master they would be just pieces of a family. Better to take a long walk and later make peace with his uncle at all costs, he thought. He wandered the woods for an hour, then turned toward Padobar.

A bearding of Spanish moss aged the town. A weather-rot town. Well water. Geriatric ghetto. The old limped around in supportive twos, or drove too close to the curb, or pedaled oversize tricycles with bells along sedate lanes. Most of these retirees lived in well-manicured trailer parks, having spread their drives, porches, and walks with consonant tidiness. They played their shuffleboard with Olympic intensity, painted their driveways with scrollwork blue, green, or gold, and gazed at people under fifty like they were runaway trucks.

At the very edge of town, the houses began, several blocks of them, all pressed forward to the edge of the road. Except for one. "Sutter," the mailbox at the curb read, but there was nothing special about the simple structure, and Kurt never noticed. He would not notice the house set back in the trees until later. He crossed the main highway where the brick and concrete buildings began. They were new—some of them—but rectilinear and without character, as if the masons had had a horror of wasting bricks. The library was one of these. He went inside.

There was just a single room partitioned with a set of perforated walls on wheels, but it held a surprising number of books. The town's aging population must have kept it busy sorting bequeathals. Kurt spoke to the woman at the desk and was shown a wall of older, mostly hardbound volumes. There were two on glass, and he took them both to a table by the window.

From the beginning he had a feeling of foreknowledge. The color plates quickened bursts of recognition. Stories, such as Pliny's of Phoenician sailors burning lumps of natron on sand to support their cooking pots and finding glass in the residue, were graphic to him. A progression of crucibles and furnaces advanced into the twentieth century for him along with familiar tools, glassmaker's tubes, pointels, and pipes. He had heard of these things before, of course, in the studio and in the kitchen from Gerta. Now with the books in front of him they seemed to authenticate each other, family and legends.

He returned the books and, from the oversize rack, picked out a religious encyclopedia that had a comparative chart of Western denominations in the middle. Under "Lutheran" his finger skated down the column to "Baptism, Communion and Other Sacraments." The last sentence read: "Confirmation is not a sacrament but a rite."

Not in the Hauptmann family.

Confirmation was a sacrament, a visible sign of the strengthening of the bond. Visible how?

▪   ▪   ▪

THE OLD MAN known as Luke Sutter was stone deaf, and he didn't hear the back door open. When he felt the first vibration, he thought it was another teenager. At least three times one of them had darted in to snatch anything of value lying around. But there was nothing of value lying around. He didn't even keep a radio or TV. They did it for bravado after the first time. He liked to sit in front of the big window in his front room and stare out at the road, and the youths could easily spot him there and go around to the back and—

It paralyzed him for a moment. The second vibration. He was no obstacle to robbery. He watched the window, that silent medium that let the world in and also reflected him sitting in his chair. He would watch them both at the same time: his reflection on the glass superimposed on the palpable world beyond. It made him look temporary, a ghost in the world of the living. And now, mirrored behind him, he watched his executioner enter the room.

It was the rope that galvanized him to action. He watched it play out in both hands of the intruder, and he struggled up and around. But his attacker seized him by the back of the neck with one hand and twisted him like a bellied-up beetle. Something happened inside his head, then. He *heard* rather than saw the window curtain knifing shut. It was the first sound he had heard in six years. The blood pounding in his skull made the darkening of the room inconsequential. Spots danced behind his eyes. A humming began, but not so loud that he couldn't hear the rope slap over the beam above his head.

The medications that held his tremors and arrhythmia in check seemed to wash away in a flood of sweat and adrenaline, and he began to void his bladder. He made noises, his eyelids fluttered, his arms jerked up and down, and when the hand on his neck was replaced by the prickly fiber of the noose, he began to march in place. But it wasn't until he suddenly sailed off the floor that he clawed and tore. A moment later the curtain slashed open.

And now those things that reached his bulging eyes were bigger than life and brighter, though dimmed at the edges. He reached for the window, the world beyond, with his right arm. There was someone passing by. A boy. A young man. He slapped at the panes, hammered with his palm. Only, he was deaf again and couldn't tell if there was a sound.

Yet the young man stopped. And then Luke Sutter stopped.

The executioner stood back from the window. He should not have opened the curtain until Luke Sutter was dead. But the association between glass windows and animated dying had been too much, and he couldn't resist juxtaposing the two while it was happening. By the time he saw the young man it was too late. The house was set back from the street, however, and it was doubtful that the event in the gloomy living room was discernible. It was only the pounding on the window that arrested the youth, who squinted for a moment and passed on. And that saved his miserable life, the executioner thought with a sense of irony, because he recognized the young man. Pulling a covered syringe from his waistband, he set about collecting a fresh sample of blood.

■ ■ ■

SOMEWHERE ALONG THE road home, Kurt noticed the house set back in the trees. There was nothing special about it, but in the front window stood a man. A nothing-special man. Just a man in a house. But the man was pounding with his palm on the window.

Kurt stopped.

The arm dropped away then, and it was a peculiar movement, too fast, as if the man were trying to catch an insect. That was it. An insect. He had tried to crush it with his palm on the glass, and then had snatched at it when it flew away.

Odd man.

▪　▪　▪

"It was because of the hounds," Gerta told him later. "Your uncle wants to keep them in the chapel cellar, and he's afraid of what might happen if you go down there. Still, that's no excuse for what he did. He was drinking, of course. And Anna and I have spoken to him about it. It won't happen again." She took a step toward Kurt, pulling his head down against hers. "No grandson of mine has anything to fear from a member of the family."

She rocked him slightly as if syncopating some inner rhythm. He wanted to ask why the rest of the chapel was locked, why the window was covered, why they called a rite a sacrament in their family, and how he could be hurt by caged dogs anyway, but the rocking smothered him.

FIFTEEN

THE SECOND TIME Jack Skelote and Nora Sandles went to a show they saw *All the President's Men*. Skelote's ex-wife had read the book when they were weekending in Atlanta, and he was prepared to hate the movie. Instead, he found it riveting and afterward he and Nora discussed it all the way back to her trailer.

"If I turn on the light first, will you come in?" she asked.

"I might."

"That's encouraging. I'll throw in a double nightcap."

"Okay."

She dug the key out of her purse and unlocked the flimsy trailer door. It opened as lightly as the flap on a Grape-Nuts box. She flicked a switch.

"It's a soft light, but you'll spot me if I try to creep up on you." He looked at the floor, and she wished she hadn't said that. "What would you like to drink?"

"I dunno."

"Hmm. This is going to be tough. What do you usually drink before you go to bed?"

"Eggnog."

"Eggnog!" she hollered like a short order cook, going to the refrigerator. "Damn. No eggs. How about a glass of milk, sugar, vanilla, and nutmeg?"

"That's okay."

"Would you settle for a glass of red wine?"

"Red wine is fine."

"Feel free to smoke."

She made lots of noise with the cupboards and the glasses and the bottle, and he knew her heart was beating like a bass drum. He could feel it beating in the hermetic little trailer, relentless and full and trying to catch up with the demand, about to break into a fox-trot and—jeez, light up a cigarette in here? There wasn't enough oxygen to support a match. No wonder her husband had died of lung cancer.

"You must be *dying* for a cigarette," she said and immediately sensed she had said another wrong thing. The beat broke into the fox-trot then.

"I'm okay," he said.

She brought him the wine, and they stood there breathlessly, a pair of drums out of sync.

"Here's to us and all the ships lost at sea," she said. They drank and when the glasses came down his was empty. "By God, you drank it like a sailor," she congratulated him and poured some more.

And poured some more.

And toasted.

And poured.

They sat down on the couch and talked till one and a half bottles were empty. Then she took his hand and said: "I'm drunk enough, how about you?"

He lifted her hand and kissed it. It was kind of ridiculous. But the frost in her gray eyes melted and she stroked his hair. "I dunno," he said, sighing heavily.

But he let her pull him up and lead him down the narrow passage to the end of the trailer. They were a pair of congo drums now. The primal darkness of the bedroom promised renewal.

And then the light went on.

There were ashtrays everywhere: two on either nightstand, five on the dresser, a half dozen along the bedstead, one on the floor. The side of the bed above the one on the floor had a man's bathrobe draped across it. Everything was neat and planned and perfect.

"Make yourself at home, sailor," she said and disappeared into the bathroom.

She popped back out a minute later in something scarlet and skimpy, and he knew it would be a crime if someone didn't love her soon. She wasn't some stiff and nubile bride waiting to be acted upon but a woman in the flower of her grace, warm and flowing and tuned outward. She was the kind of woman you wanted to arouse, the kind who would register touch like a lily in the wind. He knew that. But inside, he was dry ice.

"I dunno," he said.

She should have been insulted. She should have wrapped herself up in her dead husband's bathrobe and her indignation and told him to leave. How much pride could she put on the line? But she was past that kind of vanity, too.

Skelote risked a second glance and saw the hurt. Her eyes were brimming a little, pinching a little between the brows, but her lips were puffy and tender as if she still felt sorry for him.

"I can't do it," he said miserably.

She swayed in front of him, placing her hands on his shoulders. "You don't have to do a thing, sailor. I'll get you out of dry dock. And if we sink together, we'll sink together."

"Nora Sandles, you are one helluva woman!" said Skelote's heart, but something contrary and perverse was gnawing inside it, and it feared this heat pumping at him through the scarlet tracery over a woman's thighs and the raw sensuality in her fingers eating into him. And all he could give her was pain and silence.

▪   ▪   ▪

MAD DOG SKELOTE. He didn't dare think about it.

But he thought about it for two weeks. Two weeks without calling her. The truth was that deep down, somehow, he was waiting for her to call him. Call and forgive him. Dispel his humiliation. But for two weeks no one called. Not a jingle. And then one gray morning at exactly six-forty A.M. the phone rang, galvanizing him awake.

Nora! I was just gonna call you. God, I've been a real—

He picked up the receiver.

"Hello, Lieutenant, feel like a suicide this morning?"

It was Fay Larson, the night dispatcher at the station. Skelote felt just like a suicide.

"Lieutenant? You there?"

"I'm here."

"Sorry to wake you, but Catherton says they've got a man hanging in a front window on Ringo Road and he wants you to see something." Pause. "Lieutenant?"

"If the man isn't dead yet, tell Catherton to cut him down. What's the address?"

"Seven-seven-three."

Catherton. He wouldn't be happy until he found his first homicide.

The road was straight and slick and empty. Skelote wanted to keep on driving forever. Right into the mist. But Ringo Road had a knot on it at 773. The spectators around Luke Sutter's doorway had handkerchiefs over their noses for the most part. It was just a house with a window. And in that window stood a man, very straight, staring out at the road. Only he wasn't standing. He was hanging. And the odor was three days old.

A neighbor taking out her garbage had called it in. She had seen Sutter from the road twice in the previous two days but hadn't guessed the truth until this morning. Everyone guessed the truth this morning. Even with masks on, the ambulance detail hung out on the porch. Someone had drawn the curtain across the front window. Skelote heard at least one neighborhood hound howling in the distance as he trudged in.

The room twinkled with decay. You could feel the dry heat in the air, and you walked out feeling like you were covered with fuzz and syrup. Skelote walked out five seconds after he went in.

Catherton came out on his heels.

"Did you see it, sir?"

Skelote pulled out his handkerchief, wiped his face. "See what?"

"The body."

"I saw it. I didn't waltz with it, but I saw it."

"The neck . . . ?" Catherton gestured with cupped fingers to his throat. "I'd like you to decide for yourself."

"Oh. You mean the rope. Yeah. It had a rope around it, all right. I saw that. Nice, big rope. That what you got me out here for?"

"Not the rope, sir. The claw marks. If you don't mind stepping back in—"

"*You* step in, Catherton. Pull the curtain back. I'll stand out here and look."

Catherton went in and Skelote stood on the lawn in front of the window. It was a big window, latticed in foot-square panes. One of the panes was cracked. The milky white curtain suddenly shot back, and Skelote heard the crowd at the mailbox inhale. But he didn't inhale at all. Not for twenty seconds.

The slope-shouldered corpse drooped like it was trying to keep warm, and the face looked like twisted, ghoulish balloons. There wasn't much color that wasn't blue or gray or black or some hellish hint of vermillion. He wasn't going to hang there much longer, either. Not without his torso slipping down his spine like a pair of oversize pants. That was because the flesh at the neck was separating. It looked like a toasted marshmallow with the skin flaking off.

"See what I mean?" Catherton was at his side now.

Skelote put his nose almost to the glass. "Maybe. Maybe not. Ever lift a garbage bag that's too heavy?"

"His shirt is ripped, too. I think he fought it. There was a struggle."

Skelote went on not answering.

"I think it's a murder, sir."

For just a moment the young officer made sense. Skelote stared hard at the claw marks, if that's what they were, and thought, *This man did not want to die!* But then he shook his head and leaned back on his heels. This was Padobar, Florida. Geriatric Villa. The elephant's burial ground. There was a lot of depression. The only motive for murder was robbery, and there were easier ways to kill than hoisting someone up in his front window. He was letting himself listen to an overeager rookie who wanted a crusade or a quest.

"Ever see a hanging before, Catherton?"

"No, sir."

"Well, you might think you wanted to die. You might put a rope around your neck and jump off a chair. But when your guts heaved and stopped in your chest, you'd still do what was instinctive. You'd kick your feet and claw at your neck and rip your shirt. Because while you might want to be dead, you wouldn't want to go through dying. Not that way. It's hard to say why he picked that way. Maybe he was lonely and he wanted attention. Maybe he wanted to punish himself. Maybe he wanted to indict you and me and the rest of the world for ignoring him. Still, when he dangled, he fought it. Did you look under his fingernails?"

"No."

"Well, get the body crew to cut him down and take him to the examiner. And make sure he gets to the examiner."

Looking dejected, Catherton set the cleanup in motion. There was a footstool overturned on the living-room floor that the suicide had probably used. They left it there, along with the rope end tied off on an overhead beam. Skelote turned the background investigation and notification of relatives over to Catherton and went out to eat breakfast. But he didn't eat much. He had never seen a hanging before either.

▪　▪　▪

IT WAS THE cracked pane of glass that got him to go back for a second look.

The body was gone by then, and the road in front of the house no longer had a knot in it. The door was sealed but not padlocked. He broke the seal and went inside. Death still tingled here and there, though the clammy feeling was gone. He could almost stand the odor.

There were paintings on all four walls, landscapes with no people in them. Some roses had wilted in a vase. A creche was on the mantel. No photographs anywhere. It could have been a refuge or it could have been a prison. The chair in front of the TV was well worn; so were the books beside it.

Skelote went to the window then. The cracked pane was about opposite where Sutter's shoulder had been. It refracted light sharply when you looked at it on an angle, so Skelote thought the crack was fresh. He bobbed and weaved, trying to sight into the sun through the window. When he did, the impressions came clear. Palm prints. One of them hard enough to crack the glass. It was just one hand. Sutter hadn't been able to reach it with two. And he must have been too short of air to raise his leg and try to use the lattice like a ladder, or maybe the rope cut into his neck too much when he moved that way, or maybe he didn't think of it. But the palm prints were clear. Same hand hitting again and again. Maybe as he swung. Skelote looked closely at the wood lattice above the palm prints and saw the nicks. The examiner was going to find paint chips and splinters under Sutter's fingernails, he thought, and he was about to cast his vote for that faint possibility of murder, but his gaze passed slowly around the room once more and he realized that he had been in this place many times before. It was Marcus Adler's room. It was his own. The lattice on the window made it a prison after all. And the lonely occupant had died here a long time ago. Because there weren't any mirrors.

SIXTEEN

"HELLO, FLOCK!" VINTAGE Detlef. Dramatic effect and more than a touch of sarcasm.

Mackey toggled the diamond wheel to life, purifying the air with its whine. Otto shook glass slivers out of a cutting mat. Kurt offered Detlef a cup of hot coffee as the studio master closed the door behind himself and their eyes met, steel against velvet. Detlef poured his own coffee from the percolator on the hot plate and idly lifted a claw hammer from its pegs. Then he sauntered to the rack opposite the bench where three newly cemented belt windows were drying.

"Bad color placement," he said. "The reds are too close. Here . . . and here." With the hammer he fractured two panes, creating a void of silence behind him ". . . and the yellows—weak. They should be interior colors." Three more dull cracks, one from each window. "Picture the blues here." He tapped out a circular pattern.

Mackey stiffened white at the ruin but kept his tongue; Jimmy Pelt watched sadly for a few moments before continuing to sketch.

"We'll make superior windows or we'll make nothing at all,"

Detlef concluded with a shrug. "And now, Mr. Pelt, with your permission, we'll discuss these recent sketches you've left for my approval." He tossed the claw hammer aside, yanking several sheets of saw-toothed paper out of a drawer. "Neither you nor I have ever seen a saint, but I at least have seen men die. I have never seen one die at attention. Do you imagine that it's any different with saints? These might as well be drawings of statues. They aren't fit for little white churches." The energy of his false smile suddenly went dead. "Where is the agony, the sacrifice, the meaning of sainthood? You need to read something about martyrs. Let the bones break, Mr. Pelt. Let the blood flow. It's holy blood, isn't it?" And he pulled the ebony cross with the writhing Christ from around his neck.

"It's a pity you don't do them yourself," Jimmy Pelt said coldly.

"Oh, but I have." From his own cluttered corner of the studio Detlef retrieved a pair of sketches. "You have my permission to mimic the inspiration. Trace them if you like."

The studio artist stared grimly, then handed the sketches back, declaring with quiet conviction: "You are quite mad, Herr Hauptmann."

At six o'clock, Jimmy Pelt put his brushes away, turned off the light under the glass easel, and beetled across the drive to the screen door of the house. There he rolled down his sleeves to cover his tattoos and rapped softly.

Gerta's voice floated out. "Come in, Jimmy."

He shuffled back to miss the step, shuffled in, stood in the middle of the room, shuffling.

"I'm sorry to . . . to break in like this." He looked from Gerta to Anna.

Anna raised her face. "You're always welcome in this house, Jimmy. But you're not on a social call."

He licked his lips. "I've never complained before. I don't think anyone can say I've ever criticized the studio. The studio has been my life as much as yours, if I may say."

Anna brushed an imaginary thread from her lap.

"It's very hard for me to do my work, these days. It seems whatever I do, the results don't fit the studio's plans."

"Detlef," Gerta said bluntly.

The ice broken, Jimmy turned palms up and the words flooded out: "In the name of God, I've never seen such travesties of the craft. First, he smashed three finished windows one pane at a time. The weather seals weren't even dry. Then he didn't like my sketches. 'Not enough expression,' he said. 'Statues,' he said. For- give me, Frau Hauptmann"—he turned to Anna—"but when your husband was alive he used to say, 'Jimmy, God must have helped you paint those saints,' that's how much expression they had. But now I'm told they're statues. And what am I shown by the master himself? His own renderings. 'Trace them,' he says. God forgive me if I ever commit such blasphemies. Morgue art, that's what it is!"

Gerta puckered; Anna sat quite still.

"I love the studio," Jimmy mumbled. "I've never considered leaving it. But my art is what it is. I can't change."

Anna plucked a cigarette out of the air. "You won't have to. What you've done all these years is part of the studio's foundation. We don't intend to change that."

"And Herr Hauptmann?"

"Detlef is the master," Gerta intervened. "We can't control what he thinks and says. I'm sure he'll prove a trial to us all. How- ever, as to what he does, that will not directly affect you, Jimmy. Work as you have always worked."

He stood unconcluded, waiting for her to sweep up the shattered stained glass in his memory. But the prohibition against further outrages was only hinted at.

"I'll talk to Detlef," Anna promised.

He thanked them and left.

"It's happening," Anna said bitterly.

Gerta rocked.

■   ■   ■

DETLEF AIMED THE hose and doused the hounds into a frenzy. Then he shut the water off in the slate tub across the cellar and coiled the hose in plain sight of the crates. He stood, pulling off the gloves while the last of the water gurgled out the drain. The dogs rumbled fitfully at every move.

"Sing Cerberus," he taunted them jointly, "while I paint."

Massaging his hands, he went to the easel near the door and removed the cheesecloth rag from the canvas. It was a painting of one of the chapel windows—shuttered. The wooden frame on canvas corresponded exactly with the first of a stack of shutters across the cellar near the tubs. Squeezing out his oils, he took up a finely lashed brush and, while the cellar reverberated with low disquieted growls, began to detail tortured, surreal eyes staring out fiercely between weathered slats.

The sudden blistering of the hounds into a fresh frenzy alerted him to Anna's presence a moment before she spoke.

"I want to have a word with you!" her voice strained above the uproar.

The little smile fell in place again as he gestured his openness there in the cellar.

"Outside," she dictated and turned on her heel up the steps.

Slowly he washed out his brush, wiped his hands, and followed.

She was standing at the edge of the woods a little ways from the cellar door, her back to him. The only color in the gloom came from the deep burnt gloss of her hair.

"There," he said, "now you needn't be afraid."

She spun around, hands on her hips. "I'm not afraid of them, Detlef. If I were, I'd tell you to get rid of them."

"I didn't mean *them*."

"What did you mean, then? You? I'm not afraid of you either, in case you haven't noticed. If I were, I'd get rid of you, too."

He pursed his lips, glanced up shyly. It was a look totally out of character, and it stopped her cold. "I mean you don't have to be afraid of yourself," he said.

"Of myself?" She sounded uncertain now.

"Coming down in the cellar to see me, I mean. Alone in a man's inner sanctum. How long has it been, Anna? We've both lost someone, haven't we?"

It was the last thing in the world she expected from him, and it struck her dumb.

"I lost Eva-Marie, you lost Martin," he said, moving next to her. "I remember how I felt—the guilt for wanting someone else the first time, for wanting to go on. But you do go on. Eventually. What else is life for?" His lips moored alongside her ear, and his rough hands reached for her breasts.

In a paroxysm of outrage, she thrust him back. He was still smiling when she slapped him. And after the second slap. And the third.

"No need to rush," he said gently.

He had managed to confound her again. If she could trust her emotions, she couldn't trust her words. Shaking her head, she hurried back to the house, and it was an hour before she remembered Jimmy Pelt, or why she had gone to talk to Detlef in the first place.

▪ ▪ ▪

Dampness softened the "brr" of cicada and turned head-lights on the road into phosphorescent globes. A gossamer weave snared moonlight between chapel and pines. Ute was watching it from her window when her uncle passed down the drive. He had leather gloves on. Through the pines he went, emerging on the cellar side of the chapel. Moments later the halting sum of two shadows moved unevenly back up the drive. Behind her uncle, almost crawling at the end of a chain, was one of the hounds. Playing out the extra length in his hand, Detlef wrapped the last dozen links around the studio-door handle, padlocking the overlap. The hound backed off again, keeping the fullest possible distance. Ute thought she understood how it felt. And as her uncle turned again down the drive, she saw the smooth round club in his hand.

The whole procedure was repeated with the brindle, the dog half loping, half cowering. But this time they passed behind the studio where the chink and buzz of chain running out told her he was tethered there. Then the other black was hauled up, and this one was chained to the chapel door.

Below Ute at its post outside the studio, the first animal ghosted forward, ingot eyes embering straight up at her window. Recoiling, she scurried to bed. What was suddenly so important about the studio that they had to have watchdogs? Downstairs the screen door nipped twice, opening and closing as Detlef returned. His boots passed through the lower rooms, stopping in the rear of the house. Bedsprings compressed. One of the boots thumped to the floor. Ute listened for the second, but it never came. Maybe it was the club that had thumped, she thought, and promptly fell asleep.

For an hour the house ticked and settled, until just after one A.M. deep baying broke out. Sluggishly they all responded, drawn to the windows in time to see Detlef hurrying through the sentinel pines. By then the hounds at the studio were howling in concord. German obscenities reverberated in the emptiness on the blind side of the chapel. After that it was all a medley of snarls and chain thrashing, until the assault in the hound's voice broke. There were four poignant yelps, then a gurgle, then a cough, then nothing.

One by one the watchers returned to bed. It was a long time before Detlef returned, but they were all still awake to hear him wheezing up the drive. The black sentry in front of the studio stirred slightly and issued a very low one-note warning. Then the screen door nipped again. Soft, self-conscious steps to the bedroom. Bedsprings. Boots. Two this time. A final cough. Sleep.

It was dawn before the final disruption. The brindle this time. One J-shaped howl, dipping into its throat and rising to a glassy pitch. Ute buried her face in the pillow as the second hound picked it up. She waited for the third, and when it didn't join in, she blinked out of the warm downy hollow. The sun was just reaching for the Christ writhing on her wall. As before, Detlef thundered out of the house. Now her mother would see what a problem the hounds were, she thought with grim satisfaction. And then it occurred to her that maybe her cats had come back. Flinging the covers off, she darted to the window.

The big black hound was at the corner of the studio as far as his chain would reach, facing the road to Padobar. She looked past the flat brown grass of the cemetery and the abrupt aluminum fronts of the first trailer park to the empty yard of Luke

Sutter's house set back in the trees. A crimson pulse radiated there. She looked again to the hound. He couldn't see that far. There had been no siren.

What could he possibly be reacting to?

▪ ▪ ▪

HAVING ONCE LAIN down, Luke Sutter would lie for eternity. He would lie in the ambulance, the morgue, the autopsy room, the grave. Now he lay on the medical examiner's slab where Skelote had signed him over, waiting for the routine autopsy to verify what was obvious. His head was black and swollen, his neck vertebrae dislocated. No cosmetology for Luke Sutter. Even without the autopsy, the lid on the casket would have been closed.

The pathologist's gloves slipped on with a latex squeal.

He did the outside first, head to toe. The scrapings from the fingernails went under the microscope. It was all there. Paint flecks, skin, wood, even the cotton fiber from the shirt. It took more than an hour for the examiner to finish the preliminary, but he got enough tissue for a match-up. By then he was satisfied.

No surprises on the outside.

Rapidly he made the transverse incision across the torso. He thought he understood men like Luke Sutter. The operative theory was Loneliness. They got past talking about it and some of them did this. What lay here now in the autopsy room was meat, the same cut of meat he had seen half a hundred times. The very dryness and wornness of it connoted abandonment.

Peripherally he noticed the mark. A tiny pinhole above the heart. It had happened after death, judging by the tumescence. It could have been an adrenaline injection—if they had gotten to him soon enough—or a brash attendant's med studies, or police lab tampering. But they hadn't gotten to him soon enough. Still, the examiner was sure the pinhole hadn't figured in the cause of death.

He let the suction trocar perform its insolence. Half of Luke Sutter was in the sink.

Loneliness, thought the examiner, peeling off the gloves. He tossed them in the foot-pedal basket, drew his pen from its vest pocket caddy, and scratched a vapid obituary on a notepad. The fingernail scrapings got half a page in the final typing. No mention was made of the pinhole.

Luke Sutter would lie for eternity.

SEVENTEEN

"Did you get any sleep?" Kurt asked her with genuine concern.

"A little," Ute said. "What about you?"

He leaned back on the porch rail. "Not much after the dogs started. Funny, because my sister used to say I could sleep through Christmas."

"Maybe that's what kept you awake—thinking about your sister, I mean." She was looping a garland of evergreen boughs from the porch overhang.

"Me? Homesick?"

"Well, it *is* Christmas Eve."

"It doesn't feel like a holiday, but not because I'm homesick. I miss the snow, that's all. How can it be Christmas Eve with no snow? In Germany I'd be shoveling the walk this time of day."

"Did you like shoveling the walk?"

"No."

She gave that a soft syllable of laughter and lowered her arms, and that's how she caught him staring at her breasts again. "What *do* you like?" she asked ambiguously.

He shrugged, averting his eyes. "We used to look at family albums on Christmas Eve. Mostly they were pictures of you—I mean of all the Hauptmanns."

She raised her arms again, looping the garland rather slowly, as if inviting his stare. "Really? Then you've probably seen more family pictures than I have. I'm like Grandmamma. She has no patience with photographs. Life is for living now."

"But you're interested in the past. Grandmamma says you're already the keeper of the archives."

"That's different. That's protecting the flame. Pictures are . . . frivolous. Usually. Stupid grins and poses."

"What about pictures in stained glass?"

She glanced down again, and this time he was looking into her face. "I don't make stained glass," she said crisply.

He took a minute to gather his answer. Then he said: "Photographs can protect a flame, too. Even frivolous ones. I never would have known what Uncle Martin was like if I hadn't seen pictures of him fishing or smoking his pipe while he played the piano. And I never would have known that you braided your hair when you were twelve. Or that you collect feathers to make into fans and things. I probably never would have wanted to come here . . . or give you this."

She was distracted momentarily by the untwisting of an evergreen bough from its supporting wire, and by the time she secured it, he was gone. But there on the porch rail were a dozen white egret feathers.

He circled through the orchard and the pines to the chapel, smiling when he heard her phantom "Thanks!" called blindly into the air. Idly he paced the length of the west wall, the breeze stirring his short, blond hair and drying the humidity that glossed the flat planes of his face. There was nothing extraordinary to see.

Only an old boarded and overgrown cistern near the pines at the back. And claw marks. The hound had torn up a considerable crescent of turf at the end of its tether. Kurt's eyes walked up and down between these two features on the otherwise even terrain, making an inspired jump to the fence and the woods beyond. The thicket swirl was broken at one point, as if the hound had clambered through.

Turning back, he saw the ladder, only this time he noted the new chain and eyelets securing it to the chapel masonry. By association it drew his gaze to the six stained-glass windows in the west wall, and there, to his surprise, was a second shutter as old and rotted as the first. He walked around trying to peer through the weather-beaten slats. But if there was any stained glass, the sun through the eastern side was too weak to illuminate it.

Shoving his hands in his pockets, he crossed back through the orchard, where Ute's lithe figure flickered through the branches. Now that the hound song was reduced by one-third, she was one-third happier, having renewed her efforts to entice back her cats with dishes of tuna. Each time she found the dishes empty, she called and called, but the only animals within earshot were the shameless bandits half-mad in the hollows of trees waiting for another crack at the tuna. There was only one possible gift for her, he decided, and late that afternoon he went out and got it and returned to Christmas Eve dinner in eighty-one-degree weather.

"Is this what you mean by holiday warmth?" he asked, undoing the top button of his shirt.

"Sit down, sit down," Anna said, "the warmth is about to begin."

The evening celebration was traditional in the family on both sides of the Atlantic, and Kurt began to feel the holiday spirit for the first time. A feasting look flared briefly when the great bronze bird arrived, glistening bullishly, drumsticks goring the air. But Detlef set to it without waiting for prayer, his every gurgle, chew, and syllable of breath audible.

"Have the young craftsmen learned rapidly?" Gerta asked to break the ice.

"The technology," Detlef said. "They've learned the technology but not the art."

"That's not so bad," Anna took up. "For such a short time."

"Not bad." Detlef speared a glacial chunk of dark meat. "That's why I'm recommending regular wages for them."

Kurt dropped his fork and everyone looked up.

"Glass sliver," he apologized, flexing his fingers. "I can't find my gloves."

"I'll get you another pair," Detlef promised.

"Can we afford to pay them wages?" asked Anna. "Mother Agnes is complaining about the Magdalene panel in the order for the Marygrove convent. She said it was much more secular than the sketch. We may have to take it back. If we keep doing orders twice, we won't be able to pay anyone."

"What do you expect from a bunch of unopened bottles like the sisters of Marygrove?" scoffed Detlef. "A little loin-pounding would make them appreciate a prostitute like the Magdalene."

The silence round the table was not altogether shock. Virulent monologues had intruded on the family's most idyllic moments lately. Gerta came to grips with it this time.

"You might scrape the bottom of your heart for a little good-will at Christmas, my cynical son."

"What 'goodwill' have the Catholics ever shown us? Maybe we should send the sisters a panel of Nicholas. Now there's a saint we haven't caught in glass. Shall we model him after a fat man in red flannel, or Pope Nicholas the First, or maybe *old* Nick?"

"I think we ought to exchange presents now," Anna said, and Ute promptly began distributing the gifts from under the little tree, while Kurt slipped upstairs.

She was waving her wrist, graced by a new watch, when he returned. Slowly he brought his hand out from behind his back. A hush prevailed in the winking of the tree lights, broken by Ute's cry as she extended her fingers to the tiny ball of fur. "A Persian!" she gasped. But her eyes suddenly welled with tears, and springing to her feet, she fled lightly upstairs.

"It's Tabatha and Buttons," Anna explained to crestfallen Kurt.

"I . . . didn't mean they wouldn't come back," he said.

"Enough of presents for the moment," said Gerta. "We haven't had the toast yet."

Anna went to the *Kunstschrank* for the decanter. Removing the glass stopper, she began to pour red wine at the sideboard. By the third glass she sensed the hush of something going on behind her back. Finishing the pouring, she turned, and there was Detlef in her chair at the head of the table. Just like him to pick the most outrageous moment to challenge her. And it was a challenge, despite the mischief in his smile. If she made a scene, he would say it was a joke; if she took another seat, he would never again relinquish it. And they were all watching to see where the power lay. Even Gerta. So Anna handled it by not taking a seat. Setting the tray of glasses mid-table, she lifted one high.

"To Christmas Eve."

But before the glass reached her lips, Detlef issued a counter sentiment.

"To the old festival," he said in a voice groaning like ship's timbers, "the return of the burning wheel. The winter solstice. And to

Martin's death, and Hans's—those shocks that drove us together, the way they did when the Puritans persecuted us, and the Inquisition, and other enemies, long, long before that."

A wave of chill fear stroked white across Gerta's face. Anna closed her eyes.

Christmas was going to hell.

▪ ▪ ▪

LATER, UTE CAME to Kurt's room to apologize about the kitten.

"It just reminded me, that's all," she said and stood on tiptoe to kiss him.

The feather touch of her lips and the jade languor of her eyes stunned him. Afterward he stood a long while at his window, contemplating Christmas Eve without snow. And in the starlight, as he turned to go to bed, he noticed something odd about the chapel. There was a third shutter next to the other two, and through the mottled white slats he could see parallel lines of bright crimson.

▪ ▪ ▪

LATER STILL, GERTA and Anna took a walk.

"When was the last one?" from Anna.

"Two hundred years ago. Nearly that. Ultrich Guenther."

"Then it's real."

"Of course it's real."

"Like a germ lying dormant."

"You knew." Gerta's scowl came out somehow in her voice. "You knew when you married Martin and went through second confirmation. We've always been prepared, since the beginning, long before Ultrich's time." Looking straight ahead, she recited in German:

"How old is the family?
Old as the Fall,
Old as the night o'er the top of
the wall."

"Is Detlef the one?"

The ancient face looked papery in the moonlight. " '. . . He shall be known by his eye, his deed, and the fullness of his taint.' "

"Then what will we do?"

The question was more than a concession. It was a passing of authority.

"We shall wait," Gerta replied, "and we shall watch."

A meteorite scratched the night sky, and the oranges, which came in at Christmastide, looked like black ornaments hanging in the orchard.

EIGHTEEN

THE FIRST QUART of eggnog showed up on Nora Sandles's porch twelve days before Christmas. A local market delivered to shut-ins and she assumed it was their mistake. The next morning there was another quart, so she tried to find a number for the market, but it was unlisted. The thought of some semi-invalid assigned a quart of eggnog a day by their doctor to cure hemorrhoids was too much for her, and the third time it happened she went around to three trailers with the same lot number on successive streets. One occupant wouldn't answer the door, one wasn't home, and one talked to her for half an hour about a fat-free diet. At the end of eleven days she had eleven quarts of eggnog. And on Christmas morning Jack Skelote showed up holding the twelfth cupped in both hands like it was a partridge in a pear tree.

"Merry Christmas," he said. "If you want me to go, it's okay."

She suffered a sudden pang of remorse. "You probably don't even have antifreeze in your sleigh," she said. "Anyway, you've got more eggnog to drink than you can possibly imagine."

He went in and stood looking at the tinsel tree on her counter a long time, like he was trying to be moved or to remember something. "It isn't much of an apology," he said about the eggnog.

"It's the best apology I ever got."

"Sometimes I'm a—"

"Yeah."

"Well, I also thought . . . maybe we could pick up where we left off?"

▪ ▪ ▪

SHE CAME OUT of the bathroom in a nightie. It was on the modest side for Frederick's of Hollywood, but even at that he could see she had nipples like pencil stubs and the feminine grace he had longed for ever since the last time.

He had been dieting and doing sit-ups for twelve days but elected to remain under the covers for her entrance. With Claudia, he hadn't much bothered to embroider the urges or care how he looked. Like the time he had run a skein of red yarn through the house from the living room to the bedroom. She was supposed to follow it when she came out of the kitchen. He had lain on the bed naked, the other end of the yarn slipknotted around his scrotum and penis. He could see now that it wasn't all that erotic. A big fat man lying on the bed with yarn tied around his wang. Cute maybe, but not erotic. Claudia hadn't said a word, just gave the thing a god-awful yank all the way from the living room. He had purple plums for a week. One hundred percent effective birth control.

The Christmas lights winking in the front room of the trailer reached all the way down the hall and made the gloom shift red, green, yellow. Nora Sandles's flaxen hair caught each one like polished brass. She held his head in her palms and guided his mouth. He felt as if he were a surrogate, some lucky, virginal soul receiving initiation into the meaning of all his pent-up urges. It hadn't been this good when he thought he was in love.

With the covers roasting them, and her flimsy attire lying twisted somewhere near her ankles, he commenced the liquid fondling that brought her to short, hard gasps and thereupon entered her. Her climax lasted through a dozen surges, waned, contracted a final time, then dissolved completely. She wrapped herself lovingly around him while he went relentlessly on.

. . . and on.

. . . and on.

"What's the matter?" she murmured.

And that was when he gave up.

"I dunno."

"You want me to do something?"

"No. Wouldn't do any good."

He rolled onto his back and put his arm over his face. The Christmas lights blinked cheap neon promises. Time cooled, then froze into rigid seconds.

"Maybe you still have some bonds," she said then, "some loyalties to your ex. Maybe you need to ask her permission."

"I'll lay eggs first."

"I'm not a psychiatrist."

"Right."

They lay there for half an hour before the ashes quit throbbing, and by that time he had a rationale in place. Throw a divorce at him and a new female relationship and he was bound to make too much of it. Everything was emotions lately and there hadn't been enough action in his life to anchor him. A winter of in-activity—one suicide, a couple of accidents, some shoplifting. What he needed was a good crime wave. A really premediated evil.

Up curtain!

NINETEEN

Quillacoochee Road was an old Seminole trail, and it ran in and out of Cicadia, Marlo County's second largest town, at the north end. For twelve miles to the west it bowed slightly before skewering less populated Norse Chapel. Along that stretch there were three crossroads, a Thriftway market and gas island, one incursion of trailers on a swampy tract known as Martha's Bottom, and a handful of dry-rot homes strung out like guard posts. The rest was patchwork woods and cypress bogs and the moist fauna within.

Paul Johnson lived in one of the dry-rot houses. He had his Indian corn and his garden and his pine needle tea. Once a month he took the Social Security check the government sent him—lime green, like ripening money—and cashed it at the Flagship Bank in Cicadia. He also had his church. That was a kind of social security, too. For a lifetime of faith he got checkers, suppers, and bingo. It was tedious sometimes—gabby female hypochondriacs cornering him after sixty-six years, checkers games so methodical that for all intents and purposes they were over after the second move—but no one bent his arm to go.

On the afternoon when he went to set up the chairs for the pancake supper, he had the feeling that he was being followed. But when he stopped and turned, there were only the Muscovy ducks hissing toward him for food, one with a piece of Spanish moss dangling from its leg. He stood a moment, pretending he had something in his hand, while the ducks wagged their tail feathers and raised their crests with each false gesture. Then he continued on.

It took twenty minutes to set up chairs, but he changed a washer in the annex sink after that and counted silverware for the budget committee's inventory. Then he played cards for an hour or two, and finally one of the Ruth Circle deaconesses brought over a pot of reheated beans and they all had dinner. That left dishes. Talk. Checkers. When he left the church for home it was dusk.

And the feeling returned. Just before the edge of town. A presence. Behind him.

He stopped, sharing the last streetlight with a mole cricket whose prehistoric grotesqueness triggered a deeper unease. From the last outlying house he heard a lawn sprinkler picking up tempo—whir to ratchet, ratchet to whir. Beyond that, Quillacoochee Road became a black lane. Moving to the center, he walked faster. The nave of trees closed in now, celestial Gothic. And then he stopped again.

"I haven't any money!" he cried out.

The whimpering began unbidden in his throat, and he began to take little staccato steps. A half-forgotten legend about a lone Seminole spirit that haunted Quillacoochee bog stirred his memory. But the loping strides alongside him in the brush were not shod with moccasins. They were thudding into the earth, scuffing gravel, striking blacktop with a heavy slap, slap, slap . . . Gasping and quailing, Paul Johnson fell to his knees without daring to look back. Mercifully, the first blow knocked him senseless.

The stalker, wearing some sort of cowl inapt for the climate, gathered up the figure and carried it down the road toward Norse Chapel. Watery ruts in the mud led directly to a parked car. Just beyond, the limp old man was arranged chest down on a stump, head hanging over. There followed a series of mucky sounds, grisly scraping, more muckiness. Something metal knelled off the stump in the breathless leap of stars. Hanging from the predator's left hand was a black drippy thing the starlight refused to illuminate, and from his right, the serrated silhouette of a hacksaw.

TWENTY

THE WIND RATTLED the studio windows as if it wanted to take him somewhere, and that was why Kurt left at noon. Restively he had puttered through the morning's work, and restively he wandered out at lunch. A cat squirrel undulated across his path, drawing his eye up one of the live oaks to a ball of mistletoe. He wandered to the house and onto the porch, shading his eyes against the screen.

"Grandmamma?"

No answer. But he had already sensed the emptiness of the house.

There were bananas on top of the refrigerator. He took one on the way through and ascended the stairs, intending to go to his room. Only he didn't want to go to his room. He just wanted to meander, to move in the stultifying air, to discover some variable to what was becoming routine. And that was when he caught the asymmetry of the attic door slightly ajar. He had never been up there. The opportunity lay lazily between an inviting doorway and the unused minutes of an unspecified hour. He thumped the door all the way open and looked up the dozen wooden steps. It didn't promise much. Dust. Relics. Someone else's memories. Still, one of those things to be explored in the settling out of one's environment.

But it was not the musty old place filled with shadows and forbidden locks that he preconceived. On the contrary, it was quite dry and sun-shot. The light entering one of two quatrefoil windows at either end spangled off a galaxy of dust particles revolving in the sudden draw from the stairwell. He felt like a moist giant among arid ruins.

The dust-stars continued to rush out of his way at each step. Beneath that soft furor boiling up in his face, he tasted the wood. An architect hides his travesties in the attic of a house, truncating this beam and that. Like an X ray, the structure presented itself to Kurt in skeletal joists, bent nails, the red gummy saliva of the studs, and the knotholes in the rafters, trailing wisps of dark damp grain like blood. For all that evidence of protoplasm, he still tasted dryness. Sharp angles shaped the room, accommodating the external anomalies of the house. Space vectored. He was in a capsized ship whose hull peaked overhead.

Some of the furniture was elaborately carved. The intaglio had a distinctly religious character. Cruciform lapses marked the uprights of a narrow black oak desk similar to a lectern. At its foot was a kind of ribbed chair that flowed together like a cup. These were an ambo and a faldstool—dead names for forgotten objects. He knew only that they were old, much older than the two bentwood chairs that sat conversationally to one side.

His eye fell on the books—histories, technical works, philosophy, art. A pile of catechisms and sectarian luminaries awakened his curiosity. Some of these were leather-bound, some just loose sheets of old printed tracts without copyrights. The Vedas. The Code of Hammurabi. The Koran. Zoroastrianism. There were studies of heathenism, cults, the occult. He picked up a ruby leather volume and read a brief but disgusting account of what were called the "convulsionists," a fanatical mob of devotees who had incited themselves to perversion and madness at the gravesite of a young Jansenist, Francois de Paris, in 1727. Next he was arrested by an explanation of religious and spiritual interchangeableness in Krafft-Ebing's *Psychopathia Sexualis.* In the lore of chasm-leaping from man to God, his startled young eyes devoured the accounts of sect after sect, and collectively in that brief hour they began to twist the history of mankind in his mind.

Or was expurgated history the distortion?

There was so much incredible evil. "God rules the upper half, Satan the lower organs of the body—therefore, to each his due," was the credo of the Paterniani. Another, the Beghardi of Germany, reasoned that the soul was so transcendent, the corruptions of the flesh could not possibly affect it. Fourteenth-century Lothardi lived morally above ground, but enacted murder, perversion, and suicide with abandon underground, because that was the Devil's realm. And Carpocrates of Alexandria had advocated capitulation to malignant demons in early Christian times. Kurt took a deep trembling breath, groping into the boxes beneath the books.

Here, in a rosewood case, he discovered a sheaf of woodcuts on age-stiffened paper that traced the steps of cathedral window-making during the Middle Ages. Again he felt the strange intrusion of genetic memory that had affected him in the library. The first cut showed a churchyard with kettles of sand, lime, and soda.

A workman was blowing a cylinder of glass through a long thin pipe, to be flattened into a sheet. Kurt *knew* it would be flattened into a sheet. "No thicker than the quick of your littlest fingernail," came to him from somewhere. He searched the written legend for a source that said this, but there was only a listing of pigments: blues, reds, sapphires (which were really greens back then—and how had he known that?), and golds. Across the courtyard, artists were scraping chalk on long tables to be mixed with water. The design would be worked in wet paste.

The second cut showed glass being split by lighting an oiled string over the design, then plunging the glass in cold water.

The third was a copy of a window itself, richly bordered like a Persian rug. Mother Mary was featured in prayer, surrounded by blue—blue had been the light-gatherer in that age of glass. The framework, Kurt knew, was iron not lead. On the reverse side, in a black ink hand flowing roundly between firm slashing diagonals, was a series of pigment formulas. He had some difficulty reading the archaic German, but he knew from listening to Jimmy Pelt and Gerta the importance of these early recipes to the glassmaker's art, and he labored through the first out of curiosity:

> Kundmann received the formula for bone glass from Kunckel, and when the burial site of the heathen Lycians was unearthed in Breslau, he commissioned such glass from the fusion of sand and those bones, thus causing the heathens to suffer in the glass furnace as they had suffered at the stake . . .

The scene depicted in the woodcut must have been twelfth or thirteenth century, he realized, while the event described on the back probably took place hundreds of years after. Was the piece of stiff paper in his hand an original woodcut? It must be extremely valuable. Surely Gerta and Anna knew . . .

Oblivious to passing time, he lifted the rosewood case off a second wooden box. This one bore the Trinity in four separate inlays. The grain of the Latin cross was white wood, possibly pine, oiled and aged light yellow. A like grain of sandalwood marked the left transverse extreme with an inlaid circle, the crown of the vertical was warm cerise—perhaps mahogany—and the right extreme was ebony. He raised the lid in both hands and age wafted out. Across the mast of the vellum page on top was a hand-lettered word he had never seen before: HAGIOGRAPHY. The first letter was illuminated in blue and gold. Despite the texture of the paper, he guessed that it wasn't as old as the woodcuts. But the page following announced the text as:

> . . . being a faithful reproduction of the *Philocain,* a Roman Church calendar of A.D. 354, and of the *Usuard,* the ninth-century Benedictine martyrology, and certain other facts about the lives of the Saints.

"It's a copy, of course," tinkled lyrically at his shoulder.

He dropped the vellum and spun around.

Ute stood there, red hair aflame in the sunlight coming through the quatrefoil, her strong mouth puckering not unlike Gerta's, or rather the handsome woman Gerta had once been.

"Neat stuff up here," he said lamely, his fingers twitching as if to remove traces of dust.

She let him twist in the breeze while her gaze trickled around the attic. "If you like antiques." Her eyes met his and the green thinned out. "The family papers are more interesting, though."

"I wasn't snooping. I just happened to get into the books—" He broke off for dignity's sake. "Some of these things must be worth a lot. Don't they know that?"

"Gerta knows. If you ask her what they're worth, she'll ask you what you're worth. I snooped through everything years ago."

"You read this stuff?"

She shrugged. The Persian kitten knifed softly past her bare leg. "They're our heritage. Glass art, German thinkers, history, religion—"

"Religion? People drinking pus and eating corpses?"

She didn't react at all, and that bothered him. He couldn't tell whether she didn't care or didn't know, or knew so much more that it all came out justified in the end.

She ran her fingers around a block-front desk behind the ambo and faced him again holding the kitten in one hand, the other hand planted like a pianist striking a major chord.

"I've been translating old family rhymes," she said, plucking a drawer out by its brass knob. "They were part of this."

His blue eyes clouded. Beneath a half-dozen couplets in German on the sheaf of papers she brought out were several schematic drawings. "These are cathedrals in France and Germany," he observed.

"And England. They're all on the same axis. They're based on the megalithic yard and their axes align with the 'eye of the bull' where it was about 1500 B.C."

"The eye of the bull?"

"In the constellation Taurus. Aldebaran. The eye of the bull was important in ritual sites like Stonehenge."

He blinked rapidly, shook his head. Some of what she had said was written under the drawings, but what was she implying?

"You aren't trying to say that these cathedrals go back to 1500 B.C.? *Christian* cathedrals and . . . and the architecture? That's ridiculous!"

Green eyes simmered patiently. "Well, at least you can see the *im*possible," she sniffed. "Would it help if I told you that ox bones have frequently been uncovered at these sites, particularly in the rebuilding of cathedrals that have burned? Ox bones . . . Taurus . . . the eye of the bull? What it means," she sighed at last, "is that these cathedrals are built on pagan worship sites."

"I suppose it's more of the Hauptmann archives on religion," he passed off carelessly. "The family obsession."

"We've always served religion. With the craft. It didn't start with Ninety-five Theses nailed to a door. Grandmamma says that God arrives with every religion. You shouldn't make fun of us, Herr *Nehmer*. When you go through second confirmation you'll have a broader concept of God!" The sting of that sang in the tight repercussions of the attic, while she stroked the kitten. "We've survived a lot. You'll learn that at second confirmation, too, and it will give you a feel for time. Time is justice, in a sense. Things that are horrible get straightened out in time. Even big things."

"Like the Inquisition?"

"Time has settled with the Inquisition. We were persecuted then, but we survived. Nothing that mattered then matters now. There's a kind of peace in knowing that. It can help you endure anything, do anything. Let me show you something. I translated this two days ago."

He leaned over her shoulder and read:

How old is the family?
Old as the Fall
Old as the night creeping over the wall.

And another:

Lactantius, the early saint, declared in pious Latin
The Trinity upon the Cross is Father, Son, and
    Satan.

He pointed. "Somebody really said that?"

"Lactantius. I looked it up to make sure I wasn't screwing up the meaning. 'Father, Son, and Satan-Lucifer,' is what he said. I couldn't get Lucifer to rhyme."

She waited to be complimented as his eye picked out still another:

Ultrich had a wife, had a daughter, had a knife.
Now the blade is wet and red, wife and daughter
    lying dead.

"Cute. One of our direct ancestors?"

"Ultrich Guenther."

"Sounds like Uncle you-know-who."

"Guenther came at the wrong time. If it had been a generation when the family was hated, he would have been a catalyst."

"A catalyst for what?"

"For the old rites and ceremonies that kept us together, the ones that helped us survive the persecutions."

Their faces were enclosed in an aura of heat and lemony soap. The words tumbled out meaninglessly, faintly flavored with the vanilla taste of banana and toothpaste.

"Birth defect," he buzzed about fading Guenther.

"Congenital."

"May he rest in peace."

His lips caught the swell of hers and pressed in—resilient, hot, moist. Green jade fires banked under cushiony lashes . . . two, three, four seconds. And while excitement kicked the air out of him, numbness flooded up his neck and murmured behind his ears. He could feel the heat from her temples and a single strand of hair teasing his cheek.

Then the kitten hooked a claw into his shirt as if to pull it off. Its serpent pupils seemed to conspire with the temptation stirring in his loins. *This is my cousin!* he reminded himself, staring down into feline eyes that cushioned shut as if from some overpowering pleasure.

Guenther . . . Detlef . . . the attic full of bizarre and arcane documents all seemed like precedents for something unholy and passionate. He didn't dare think ahead. It wasn't incest to place his hands heavily on her shoulders and slide them down, was it? It wasn't incest to knead the yielding flesh and draw the turgid nipples to points? And then to unbutton her blouse . . . and uncup her delights . . . and tease them with his tongue?

She stood paralyzed with desire and shock while he performed these things. And when he slid his right hand into her jeans, she closed her eyes and gasped at intervals while he provoked her to the dew point.

And then he stopped.

They stopped.

She stood there, half-melted, unable to sanction or rebuke him.

He fled, heart pounding, out of the attic, bearing an indelible image of startled green eyes, delicate distending nostrils, and puffy red lips back into the cool of the day.

TWENTY-ONE

SKELOTE COUNTED FROGS splattered on the highway and tried to remember what his daddy used to say: "They aren't really splattered, they're just . . ." The frogs took a beating every night on this road. It was the same road where Paul Johnson had been found with his head sawn off, upstaging the frogs. *They aren't really splattered, they're just . . .*

He was on his way back from Cicadia. Two brutal murders in separate parts of the county were on his mind. The second one had brought representatives from every police department in Marlo to Cicadia, Skelote inclusive. The sheriff's department had jurisdiction, but Cicadia had found the body. Crimes always got assigned to towns, or they got ignored. Nobody counted dead frogs splattered on a highway. *They aren't really splattered, they're just sleeping inside out.* That was what his daddy used to say.

So, Cicadia and Palm Hollow had a little panic going, and the other departments in the county knew there was a repeater loose and had come to learn what there was to learn, which wasn't much. Old white men were sleeping inside out in Marlo County.

Skelote thought he had a head start on it, but the phone was already ringing off the hook when he got back to Padobar. There were the garrulous types wanting a readiness report, the fearful types reporting shadows, and The Pearl Acres Trailer Park Citizens Crime Watch Committee. Alma Pendergast on Third Street saw a suspicious-looking man buy a new hacksaw blade at Durham's Hardware. Skelote assured her the killer would only use old, rusty hacksaw blades.

Then there was Chief Wagner.

" 'Lo, Jack? Harry. What are we doing about these homicides?"

"Nothing."

"Oh. Well, why aren't we?"

"They're not our homicides."

"I'm getting calls, Jack. Our citizens are frightened. They're asking me to do something."

"Go ahead and do something."

"What?"

"Damned if I know."

"Are you going to do something?"

"Not a thing."

"Jeez, Jack . . ."

It ended like that. Not being the drum major could be nice, Lieutenant Skelote thought.

▪ ▪ ▪

ENTER TOM DUFFERSON, middle-aged, living on the eastern arm of Quillacoochee Road out of Cicadia, surrounded by his dairy farm, a wife, three children, and a border collie named Sentry. Every evening since Paul Johnson's decapitated corpse was discovered, they knelt together and prayed for the murdered men's souls, the murderer, and their own safety through the night. The last prayer was always answered, and on this particular morning, Tom Dufferson rose up again at dawn hale and hearty.

"No mist," he heard Shellie breathe in her cottony voice as light wedged into the room from beneath the lifted shade. He felt her clamber over the mattress and lie across his back. "Plain or raisin toast?" buzzed against his shoulder.

"Raisin."

His big neck squinched up as she blew on it. Then he got up and dressed. One of the boys was stirring across the hall. Avoiding the floorboards that creaked, Tom Dufferson went into the bathroom, urinated, examined a sore spot on his lip in the mirror, and started out into the hall.

"Want some help this morning, Dad?"

Bruce swayed sleepily in his jockey shorts.

"Go back to bed," Tom Dufferson said. He was pleased with the offer, but until basketball season was over and the boys could get their studying done at a decent hour, school mornings were for sleep.

Shellie had four burners going already, and the bacon sounded as garrulous as the henhouse. Yesterday's crumbs were burning in the toaster. He stuck his finger in the raspberry jam, and his wife slapped it with a spatula. Tom Dufferson went out of the house grinning.

The rich, moist mud in the yard curled up to the barn. It had the cold, settled look of morning. He fastened the neck button of his shirt, leaving steamy footprints as he crossed to the pasture. Despite what Shellie had said when they awakened, there was a mist. A "chicken spit" mist, locals called it. He walked the dead furrow of the half-acre field behind the pole barn and opened the pasture gate.

The lead cow stood on the far border of the lemongrass plot, but though he whistled and hooted she remained stock-still until the moment he slapped her rump. Then she started out with a little shudder and the rest of the small herd wended after her. His practiced eyes read their markings like a roster, came up one short, and darted to the thin flanking woods. "Hie, hie!" he shouted, catching sight of the stray within the trees.

But the stray didn't move either.

He trudged to the edge of the wood. Why and how the lackadaisical animal had gotten itself into all that fallen scrub and mud aroused no curiosity in him. It was always so with cattle. Usually his breaking of brush and the sucking in and out of his boots in the muck would stir a cow, but this one made no effort to free herself, as if she were tethered—which was absurd, of course.

Except that she was tethered.

And that single burst of truth expanded his peripheral vision to the rag of steamy breath within the leaves to his left and the unweathered whiteness of a sharpened wooden shaft sticking out. He tried to slide his feet, but the mud held them, and he grabbed wildly at the cruel thrust of the spear. In the end he toppled backward as far as the shaft protruding through his body allowed.

Saucer-eyed, the tethered cow lowed uneasily and stamped her hooves at what followed.

TWENTY-TWO

UTE TWIRLED A lemon-hued feather from the mirrored tray on her dresser. Back and forth it pirouetted between her fingers, blurring gold against the light through the window. It reminded her of the dervish energy in a fine watch spring. A feather was a blend of what was most gentle and most enduring in nature. Tossed into the air, it landed safely; bent, it yielded; ruffled, it combed itself out at the first touch. She liked to float them on her mirror tray, pretending they were downy barges reflected in a silver lagoon.

Glancing down from the window, she saw Kurt wheel one of the racing bikes out of the shed. Like a skater taking a partner by the hand and waist, he walked it beneath her window and swung one leg over the seat; and in that moment she caught and held his gaze, inquiring. But neither had the courage to prolong it, and he one-footed the bike in a semicircle and went shimmering out of sight.

■　■　■

HE DOWNSHIFTED, COASTING between each click, and the air slipped round his head, cooling but not clearing his emotions.

Ute, Ute. He repeated this in rhythm, but the thin tires seemed to smear it into the blacktop with an adhesive hiss.

Guilt hadn't kept him from speaking to her. If he felt guilty about anything, it was about the family. An attic full of heresies seemed to cast the craft in a gray light. This troubled him deeply, because he wanted more than anything else to belong here.

A half block from the library he glided behind a huge wire bin truck filled with oranges, lifted the bike over the curb, and coasted into the bike rack. He knew exactly what he wanted this time. Secrets were shutting him out, and he remembered now when the secrets had begun in his life. It was at the time of the journey to the cathedral with Uncle Detlef. He had been sent from home because something was happening to Monika, of course, but there was more to it than that. Detlef had taken him and Otto to Chartres for a purpose.

Parting the glass doors, Kurt turned left into the stacks and ran his finger down the spines. There were a half-dozen volumes on cathedrals. Notre Dame, Bamberg . . . Chartres! The cover photo of this third book stirred memories: steep, twisting streets past what must have been a flour mill, small factories, and shops, then a tiny park, or plaza, brocaded with shrubs. He remembered standing with Otto and Uncle Detlef before the mighty edifice, its mismatched flanking towers built centuries apart stabbing into the sky just as the photo indicated. The three visitors must have looked like the three lancet windows—two smaller ones on either side of the larger. Above them had floated the rose window with its delicate plate tracery.

The book cover opened like the great cathedral door, twin color plates surrounding him as had the stained glass on either side. The north windows were more blue, the south flushed red and orange. The next plate was in black and white, and he remembered his eyes adjusting to the nave, a towering corridor of leaping stone that crisscrossed overhead like papery bat wings or some concave, respiring lung of ribs and membrane. Unlike the busy sculptures in the tympanum above the central portal, whose eerie, robed figures had given him the feeling he was expected here, the interior columns were almost stark and the space between filled with implication. It was like an empty house waiting to be peopled. "Do something," it said to the pilgrim. Worship seemed inevitable.

And what had they done?

He leafed through the book at a walking pace, rediscovering bursts of color in hauntingly familiar shapes. A decade of night dreams had diffused those unities and rewoven them into other images in his life, so that he felt a sense of stabilization now in the sudden coming together of his past.

The Prodigal Son window stopped him at page twenty-five. His eye skimmed immediately to a frame of the story showing the Prodigal Son dragged from his bed by devils. Uncle Detlef had instructed them at this picture, which had been banished to the north transept, unlike a similar one in the choir at Sens and Bourges.

Again, halfway through the book, he was fascinated by a series of frames of some special significance that almost triggered his uncle's words. This one contained the story of St. James. But it was the figure of a man with a little demon perched on his shoulder that riveted him. He was Hermogenes, the book said, a famous magician who had commanded demons and whom the Pharisees respected. Why was that important? The secular story of magic occupied a prominent position near the central chapel.

Kurt could conjure forth the deep rumbling voice his uncle had then, but the words were all bumbled together with the echoes, like a Gregorian chant, in and out of Chartres anatomy of stone and glass. He came to a series of structural shots—portals reamed out of the transept in concentric arches, the apse, another photo of the gaunt nave, an aerial view showing the cathedral pinned to the ground, as if by guy wires, which were really flying buttresses.

And finally, there was the crypt. A great crypt. The foundation of Chartres, heavy columned with intersecting vaults. He seemed to see behind the shadows in this picture, and below into the Gallo-Roman substructures. Again he trusted his memory to lead him to a spot on the floor, but there the flickering recollection fled. The text contained the story of Quirinus, a governor sent by the Emperor Diocletian to suppress Christianity. Among his cruelties was the torture and killing of a beautiful girl, St. Modesta, said to be his daughter. Her body had been thrown into a well along with other victims near the altar of the old worship site. The Chartres's mass still contained a reverential pause in the bishop's *Pax vobis* or the priest's *Dominus vobiscum* associated with the well.

Kurt closed the book thoughtfully. Was the spot on the floor the place where the pit was? According to the book, that well had been rediscovered in 1901 after many attempts to find it. What had Uncle Detlef told them at that point? He had made them . . . what?

The answer receded, and he heard the door to Chartres close with a terminal roar. And now he was running, running and weeping, a small boy chastised along by his uncle.

Reluctantly he returned the book to its shelf and left the library.

■　■　■

THE YARD WAS empty when he reached home, but brightly ribbed lawn chairs had been set out. A woodpecker drummed obtrusively on the dead wood of a utility pole. Kurt dropped lightly off the bike and lowered the kickstand. From the studio he heard Uncle Detlef and Jimmy Pelt arguing:

"... how dull, how unimaginative. Are these the same sketches you did before? And before that, and before that—"

"Yes! The same ones that built this studio."

"The studio is merely the latest chapter of a craft that was built before your ancestors could read!"

"At least when they did learn to read, they read the Bible."

"Then your sketches are lies. Because they all say God is dead!"

From the orchard a sudden blast of guitars and drums exceeded the tolerances of Otto's cheap portable stereo. Remounting the racer, Kurt wheeled slowly toward the source.

Otto nudged the brim of a blue cap off his eyes when he saw his cousin and lowered the volume on the stereo.

Kurt lay the bicycle down and flopped onto the grass.

"Why is your father pissed off at everyone, Otto?"

"It's not everyone. Just me."

"Not true. He hates everyone."

"Supposedly he was different before my mother died giving birth to me."

"And that's why you think he hates you?"

"It's not all that subtle, and it doesn't really bother me. In a way, I've never had a father, that's all."

"I lost my father, too, Otto."

"... so the orphans went to their grandmother's in Florida and lived happily ever after."

"You fit in here," Kurt said. "I don't. You've had second confirmation. You know all the family's secrets."

"Ute said you were paranoid about that."

"Why shouldn't I be?"

"Because it's not something that matters. It's just something to pass along, like a gold watch. There hasn't been any need for it in a long time."

"Not since Ultrich Guenther?"

Otto's brow knit. "There wasn't any need then, either. Ultrich was triggered at the wrong time."

"Triggered to what? By what?"

"Hate. That's usually what threatens the family. Or a lack of belief or caring from within. Whatever might make the craft fall apart."

"But the craft is more than making stained glass to the glory of God."

"Actually, that's exactly what it is. Worship. The craft is what it is. You see what it is. We're just people getting along and not getting along. What do you want from me?"

Kurt rose, brushed himself off. "The future, Otto. The future is what I want to be a part of."

"None of us knows anything about the future." Otto reached to the stereo, and a fury of drumbeats came between them.

TWENTY-THREE

IT WAS TOO bad Skelote wasn't talking to reporters, because privately he made three predictions that were right on the money: "The lousy, shit-raking, yellow journalistic fourth estate is going to tempt this sicko, sadistic homicidal maniac to splash blood in Padobar. They're going to stir racial unrest, promote the Klan, and cause everyone to arm themselves to the teeth. And it's going to hamper law enforcement no end."

It was the racial unrest that showed up first. Padobar's octogenarians were not big on millage and the local high school was housed in an undernourished building that could only be described as early storm culvert. The kids were predominantly white, arrogant, and not particularly bright, if standardized test scores meant anything. Most of the girls cracked their knuckles, and the assistant principal issued bans, warnings, and dress code revisions from the relative security of his office. There were a lot of buttons that went unbuttoned at Padobar High.

Trouble escalated on a Friday when a mulatto girl got beat up in a locker room by the homecoming queen and two members of her court. The three assailants were white. They had earlier hung a sign on the mulatto's locker directed at her mixed parentage: SKUNK.

On Friday night the six-foot-tall black father of the mulatto went over to the homecoming queen's house and beat the hell out of her father, who stood five-seven in crepe soles. It made a lot of people edgy. Catherton arrested the black assailant Saturday morning on a complaint, but Skelote released him three hours later after the man's wife received death threats over the phone.

Harry Wagner was on the line within ten minutes: "Are you crazy, Jack? That nigger nearly killed someone last night."

"Someone's threatening to kill his wife and daughter. I figure they're in more danger than anyone else."

"A couple of crank calls, Jack. You don't release a dangerous prisoner for that."

"You want I should lynch him? You got some extra sheets and crosses over there?"

"I think you oughta remember who you're talking to," Harry Wagner said.

"Yeah, I remember. Trouble is you just can't trust the hired help anymore, Harry. If you want the job done right you have to do it yourself. You wanta do it yourself, Harry?"

Very softly the phone went dead.

A couple of crank calls! No one would have known that except the people who had phoned the death threats—the same people who had called Harry Wagner the minute Skelote released the prisoner. It sounded like the Klan. Good ol' boys. Harry Wagner probably wasn't a member. He never did his own work.

By Sunday morning there weren't any dead skunks on the roads for seven miles around Padobar. They were all on the porch of a certain black man and his white wife.

Skelote had thought a good crime wave would relieve his sexual frustration, now he needed a jolly orgy to relieve the crime wave. He could think about Nora Sandles until his underwear was all stretched out of shape as long as he was three miles away. But every time he got ready to put a move on her, it came to him how long he had been married and a few million of the subtler things that had shaped his married libido, and it seemed as if, even though he knew he was divorced, it wouldn't truly be over for ever and ever until he had a climax with someone else. It wasn't fidelity to Claudia. It was fidelity to something in himself that he couldn't give up on yet.

He had gotten rid of all Claudia's pictures a long time ago, except for one. Now he went to the nightstand, shuffled some receipts, and, by God, it was right there. He took it out and looked at it and thought: *Dammit, Claudia . . . dammit, I want permission to screw Nora Sandles.*

He thought it again.

Then he went to see Nora Sandles.

She was glad to see him. They sat for about an hour and talked. When the conversation got thin, he took her hand and kissed her. She started repeating his name then and looking worried, as if she were being persuaded against her will. That turned him on a little more.

It was okay until they got to the bedroom, where she took off her clothes for him and lay on the bed for him and beckoned boldly. Trying not to think, he was all over her passionately, hands and legs and torso. She gasped and clawed. He grunted and pawed. She triggered readily beneath his brutish thrusts, just like before. And they went on, just like before. For a long, long time. But then he petered out. Just like before.

"I'm not in any hurry, Jack," she said. "Are you in a hurry? Why should we be in a hurry? You helped me over widowhood.

You gave me courage and will and . . . and self-esteem. That took a real man, after Jerry. Believe me, I didn't want to face the world again, and then I saw you, and I knew you were lonely, and I thought we'd be good for each other. And we were. We are. You have to give it a chance."

He laughed harshly. "If I gave it any longer, I'd need a skin graft."

He went home from Nora Sandles's feeling like a big, stupid cop who couldn't score with women. Because the problem wasn't that he needed Claudia's permission to do it; the problem was that he needed to do it without Claudia's permission.

TWENTY-FOUR

THE STILL AIR seemed to be wedged between the open window and the sill and Ute's kitten mewed through the wall just often enough to intercept Kurt's sleep-bound thoughts as he worked the sheet down to his feet and back again in restless stages. He wiggled, he rolled, he kneaded out the topography. The lazy shriek of a plane scratched the night, and it seemed to him that great chunks of metal crawling through thin air were as impossible as membership in the family. Sometime after midnight the corybantic howling of the chapel hound shattered the stillness. Once only. And then, at last . . . sleep.

This time when he awoke, the cool damp air and the limpness of the sheets hinted at dawn. Had he heard the front door close? He could do nothing about Chartres, he thought, gliding to the window, but the chapel was here and now. Peering anxiously up the drive past the pines, he saw in the smoky gloom that the hound was gone, and above its watchpost, touched by a faint untraceable light, he discerned six shutters.

Throwing on jeans and a polo shirt, he checked the window once more. Ute's kitten had stopped mewing, perhaps hearing him. To avoid the brindle chained at the front of the studio, he passed stealthily through the house to the back door. It was not unusual for the chapel hound to be locked in the cellar or brought to the studio with the brindle when Detlef worked all night at the chapel. Coming around behind the sheds, he cut through the orchard to the west face of the building. There he pondered the shutters and pulled at the ladder, which was chained to the eyelets in the masonry as before. He was almost certain that the thin blade penknife in his pocket could trip the old chapel lock. But he didn't dare spend many minutes inside, no matter what he discovered. If the hound began baying, Detlef would certainly see him leaving, or if not that, find him missing from the house and deduce the rest.

For a few seconds he wavered at the whole idea. What did he expect to accomplish? This was not the Chartres of his past, even if that childhood memory did mean something. But there *were* secrets in the family . . . secrets that locked him out as surely as this door.

Leaning close, he inserted the knife blade against the weathered jamb. The bolt kept slipping back with a soft clack that must be resounding inside and through the floor to the cellar below. Why wasn't the hound reacting? He made another try, and this time the bolt cleared and the door pulled free with a rush.

Despite the streaky dawn still coagulated darkly to the west, very little light entered either by the front or through the high windows to the east. But he could smell dampness, paint, caulking, kerosene, and he knew the chapel had changed since Uncle Martin's funeral. His groping hand sought the pews, finding nothing. Something rectangular and open climbed the east wall. The floor was gritty.

Five more cautious steps and he turned around. Now the light from the door merged subtly with the faint illumination through the windows, resolving two masses of shadow. The first, on his right, were the pews, uprooted and stacked against the wall. To his left, the climbing thing became a scaffold under the unshuttered windows.

His foot made contact with the brace of a sawhorse, and the slender channeled rods of lead cames came under his touch. Unmistakably, his uncle was working stained glass. The shutters, appearing one at a time on the west face, and now the east apparently destined for the same transformation, hinted at a private masterwork in progress. And judging from the divergence in tastes between Jimmy Pelt's sketches and the kind of motifs Detlef was producing in the studio, he knew what form that masterwork must be taking. The scaffold meant that the belt windows were being mounted from inside—after the shutters were in place!

He peered hard at the black windows to the west but discerned nothing. Taking a deep breath, he turned to face the front of the chapel again.

There was another odor now, haunting, persistent. Here in the near darkness, without the encumbering dominance of senses, he slipped readily into that time lapse provided by genetic memory. The odor wafted out of his past: scorched brick . . . molten glass . . . ashes. He knew what it was. Without knowing the exact form, he knew what it was. Probing cautiously, he touched the bricks and the cauldrons where they sat on staggered levels. There was a flue leading upward, probably to the chapel venting. The altar, like the pews, had been removed. His uncle had built a rude glass furnace in its place.

He was making glass. The old way.

The hiss that writhed suddenly through the darkness constricted Kurt with ice. He spun around and at the same time cowered to one side, hoping to escape the titan silhouetted in the doorway. But his uncle grabbed furiously until he had him by the hair, the shoulder. From below, the hound's voice seemed now to add rage to Detlef's, "I should hang you by the testicles to the bell tower!"

Detlef hauled him into the light of the door, then through it to the path outside. Kurt more or less cartwheeled along, planting his feet between each thrust.

"What did you see? What did your filthy eyes see?" Detlef scarcely paused for the disavowal. "How long were you in there? Did you have a light? If I find a flashlight or even a burnt match in there, so help me I'll do to you what I'd do to an outsider."

"I am an outsider," Kurt gasped.

Detlef regarded him without pity. "You don't seem to re-member much, for a Hauptmann." And wrenching Kurt again, he made for the cellar annex.

The hound's howling sharpened when the door boomed open. Kurt was pushed down the first two steps into a cannonade of sound. Then the sliver of light collapsed like a silk fan knifing shut. Something scraped against the exterior panels.

"Spy to your heart's content, nephew! You've got the run of the cellar this time."

Dropping onto the top step, Kurt pondered the gulf leading down to a room he had seen only once, only briefly. He had to steel his courage to descend into that milieu of hostile sound and foul smells. *The hound is caged,* he told himself. *Or else it's chained.* And when he was convinced of that, convinced that the burning ingot eyes would rein up at the end of some tether, he did what he had to do. Because he wanted the light. And his fingers entered the scintillating void timidly acrawl up and down the wall's edge until he found the switch.

The light splattered on, expanding the room from the close little hell of his imagination to a mundane cellar. There was still the hose, the gas cocks, the sawdust (gray now), the chewed crates, one of which contained the hound. Gone were the tools, the shutters, and the sawhorses. His eyes homed on the bared gums and salivating jaws that kept seizing the air in anticipation.

And there was something else. Something insidious. More tattered now than when he had last seen them, but no doubt his. The one lay on the floor between the hound's forepaws, the other was tied to a broken oar handle as if it had been used to taunt the animal. Kurt stared in horror at his missing gray suede gloves.

Heeding the rapacious barking, he backed slowly up the gloomy steps again. From the cool doorway, the hound's deafening note actually made him see sparks. Bark away, he thought. Somebody would eventually investigate. The family would come for him as soon as they realized where he was. Otto and Ute might be afraid to cross Detlef, but Aunt Anna and Grandmamma wouldn't stand for it. They would come.

Slowly the sun warmed the door at his back and traffic began to pick up on the main road. Where were they? He tested the door with his shoulder. Then, smarting at his own stupidity, he remembered the penknife.

He had already opened one door with it, but like a guilty child he had been banished to a room from which he hadn't had the courage to try to escape. He fumbled for the blade. The dead-bolt catch was wide and there was ample room between the door and the frame for the knife to bite. With a little wiggling he slid the bolt back. But the door opened less than an inch and held.

The scraping sound he had heard shortly after it closed suddenly attained significance. Detlef had plunged a pin into the rusted hasp above the bolt. Angered, Kurt hammered on the panels. Below him the hound raged, but he had scarcely covered his ears when the hasp seemed to let go of its own accord and the door flew open, toppling him into sunshine and mist.

Kneeling there on the grass, he looked up uncertainly into Ute's beryl green eyes.

▪   ▪   ▪

NOT A WORD had passed between them since that afternoon in the attic. Not a word passed between them now. It seemed like they were back there, hearts pounding, bodies magnetized, the air charged and inadequate for breathing. He rose slowly to his feet while she shook her head "no." Suddenly he snatched her to him in a crushing kiss that buried forever any ambiguity.

When at last she pulled her mouth free, Ute threw a frightened glance at the house. "Not here," she gasped, and they hastened into the woods alongside the chapel.

She tried to say something else then, to slow down the pace of what was happening, but their momentum was too great, and he had her in his embrace again. Their lips and hands plied like greedy children's trying to obtain more than they could of a good thing. A blue jay shrilled accusatively from on high and shafts of sunlight broke through the branches as if to search them out. "Kurt . . ." she begged, but he bent her backward, sliding his hands down the arch of her back and over her buttocks where they met between her legs. He thrust her up against his hips. "Stop it!" she commanded with enough urgency to make him hesitate.

"If we don't do what we want to do, it won't change what we're thinking, will it?" he said more than asked. "And that's where the sin is, isn't it?"

"You can repent for your thoughts, and no one gets hurt."

"You think I'll hurt you?"

"It's irresponsible. I could get pregnant."

"You don't have to get pregnant. And what if I say I'll marry you?"

She looked at him with a mixture of surprise and doubt. "You don't love me. And how do you know I love you? Besides, we couldn't have children. Our genes would be all screwed up or something."

"In this family? What difference would it make?"

She shook her head in bewilderment, bracing her hands in the crooks of his elbows. "Why am I talking about this as if it were possible? This is crazy. First cousins don't marry."

"Funny. I've always had the feeling that I'm not really in this family." He dropped his arms. "Anyway, Ultrich Guenther had second confirmation, didn't he? This family holds insanity in rather high esteem, it seems to me. Maybe our offspring would be more welcome than you think."

"There won't be any offspring."

"No? Then you wouldn't make love with me even if you believed I wasn't a member of the family?"

"You shouldn't be asking that question."

"Prove to me that I'm in the family and I won't ask it."

She hesitated a moment, trying to see the direction he was going. He reached out and stroked her hair, as if she had acquiesced.

"I can't prove what's obvious if you don't accept it," she said and pulled her head away.

"Yes you can."

"How?"

"Make me a member now. Tell me about second confirmation."

Her green eyes darkened and the anxiety smoothed to hopelessness on her white brow.

"Explain it to me," he pleaded. "If I'm really your blood cousin, explain it to me. Tell me the family history in detail. Then I won't try to love you again. I'll . . . repent for my thoughts and just forget it. Explain it to me, Ute."

"Is that all you wanted in the first place?" she asked wearily and, turning, passed slowly out of the woods.

TWENTY-FIVE

SHEILA MASON PLAYED the radio and drove fast on Folger Road. Ever since the murders had begun she had dreaded this trip home from the nurses' night shift at Palm Hollow Emergency to her Padobar trailer. Never mind that the victims had all been men. She wasn't going to be the first woman. Every dip and hollow was opaque with leaden fog, requiring her to slow to a crawl at exactly the wrong places. It was precisely there that dawn hung its lanterns behind the flanking swamp, threatening her with silhouetted assassins. So she locked her doors and kept the windows up and endured the dreary cypress sentinels or the stretching oaks that had awakened like a drowsy firing squad just to execute her at the poetic moment of sunrise.

Infrequent crossroad lights licked her face, and she automatically glanced at herself in the mirror: skin pale, lips black, eyes like chocolate drops. When the news came on about the murders, she turned the radio off. Another vehicle passed, one of its headlights angled off the road, giving it a dull, idiot look. She drove in her stockinged feet, knees apart to purge the ache of eight hours on fallen arches. Reaching down to her right foot, she worked a toe separator loose. The engine sounded edgy in the dampness.

She passed the convenience store where, before the murders, she would have stopped for something sinful to eat. No way, now. Bad enough to return to an empty trailer and have to go through the trauma of turning on lights while she held a referee's whistle between her teeth.

Her Dodge Charger rattled percussively around West Circle Drive, the way marked by mailbox reflectors, slanted trailer number decals, and gold porch lights swimming like ill-defined moons in the fog. The left shoulder kept the woods at bay, though it was dotted with small deaths, sacrifices on the doorstep of darkness. The frogs were sleeping inside out on West Circle.

I'm going to get a dog, pet section waiting list or not, she promised herself. God, she hated living in a trailer park. Homes that could get up and move were not homes at all, no matter how radiant the deceits of flower beds and cinder-block hems. And now her own little fraud came into view on the end. Terminal punctuation. Lot 316. How had she got here? Private, the man had said. Gardens. Nice neighbor on the other side. Bullshit. Lonely . . . a jungle . . . and Mr. Tagorski (if that *was* a human being who had appeared for a week last spring and not just a mummy in progress) now lay in a Baltimore hospital where he was spending eternity while his name on the mailbox survived as circumstantial evidence. Lot 316. She coasted into the drive and turned off the lights.

It looked quiet. Hello, trailer. Are you empty? This was another part of the trauma—sitting in the car for several minutes with the ignition on, sizing things up. The woods were never quite right. Ambulatory bushes. Someone rearranged them every night while she did eight hours as an angel of merc(enar)y.

She hauled one fat leg up on the seat, massaging the foot,

though the toe separator under the stocking kept getting in the way. The lake in the woods stunk. Park sewage. The county was suing. What had she ever done to them? She never went near that cesspool. You flushed a toilet and the next thing you knew a whole county with a battery of lawyers was suing you. Just another way to become a victim.

And what was that right on the edge of the water?

Her tired eyes wrestled with an unnatural symmetry beyond the trees. Too quiet out there now. She shut off the ignition to verify the silence. No birds, no frogs, no crickets. Where were all the things that went bump in the night? Calling all reptiles. Again her eyes went to the symmetrical thing. It looked inanimate.

Fumbling the whistle out of her purse, she made the dash over pine needles to the porch. There, enlivened by the cold cement on her unshod feet, she leaned out, scrutinized. Her eyes preserved after-ghosts of a gigantic "X" as they blinked away the obscuring foliage, and her mind weighed a decision to see for herself, as if it were a game of Xs and Os: X-plore, X-amine, X-plain me . . . Outcry, Objection, Oppose.

X prevailed.

She dropped her shoes, her purse, and stepped off the porch with the whistle clamped between her teeth. The sky was lighter now. She could tell that the symmetrical thing was made of wood. Wobbling half crouched on tender feet down the twig-strewn trail, she made out that it was an "X" hewn of heavy beams and jammed into the shore. There were not more than twenty trees in the thin peninsula that eyebrowed around the small lake. Lowering her gaze, she resumed a wincing ballet down the path leading to the shore.

Had she looked up from the pebbles before she danced the final rapid steps, she might have seen what stuck up in rigid agony over the upper transversals. But she did not. And so her face was within a yard of it when the whistle plummeted with a dull tinkle from her mouth and the moan began to roll in her throat as she stumbled stiffly into the shallows, her eyelids pulsing out of control. Above her, frozen in the act of pouncing, was a man. His white fingers were contorted, his face tinged green and clenched, his eyes only gray crescents rolled back, and he was crucified spread-eagle to a St. Andrew's cross.

▪ ▪ ▪

"ANDREW RUSSELL," THE examiner wrote on the clipboard in the kingdom of the forensic pathologist. This was the room of ultimate indignities where no one protested, where death was comprehended as exploding gas, dropping temperatures, electrical leakage, and stiffening tissue.

"Body number 76–330. Temperature seventy-nine . . . at two degrees loss per hour, subject dead nine and a half hours."

Angles.

Pallor.

Blood settled to lower trunk.

Gravity would soon suffuse his back a deep violet. What were the pricks on the forearm? Insulin? Drugs? False starts of the spikes by a tormenting killer? No wonder he had died of shock and not the hemorrhaging.

Now the suction trocar. Segments of steel, rubber, one of glass. Feeding end wreathed in perforations. Sample phials set up. Sink on with a suggestive rush. To the left and a little above the vanquished's navel—*thrust home!*

The examiner's jowls quivered with the effort as the trocar sank and twisted into the stomach. Through the glass connector he previewed the sputter of brown fluid, a kernel of corn, stringy cabbage. Filling one phial, he let the rest splash into the lead sink. Hungry snake. Twisting, it ate through a garden of leafy membranes and gorged organs. The right chambers of the heart released thick black blood with a roar, while the trocar thumped ribs and spinal column like a hasty vacuum cleaner in a room full of oversize furniture. Next, it popped the gaseous pastry of the intestines, slaking off giggling juices into the sink. The examiner worked with impunity, knocking against the pelvis as he invaginated the trocar into the scrotum.

At this point, the procedure differed radically from the embalmer's art. Instead of reversing the trocar to pump preservative into the thorax, and beginning the cosmetology of sewn lips, plastic eye caps, and flesh paint, the examiner performed the private act of his office: the slash, the swordsman's ritual coup de grace from left collarbone to right hip.

When he finished with the body, he looked at the papers. There was a donor card, useless owing to the circumstances of death. Andrew Russell was good for only one thing now. The petite blond in the pathology lab office took care of the details, and body number 76–330 was sent to the basement of the medical school at the examiner's alma mater. There it was lowered into a stone tank of embalming fluid where its arteries were flooded for ballast and it swayed in seven-foot depths, supported by a kind of stethoscope plugged into its ears and attached to an overhead rod; one of a line of cadavers arrayed like an ordinal row of sport coats.

Just as well. Because someone else was not done with him. Someone who came looking for him after searching in vain for funeral notices and checking out cemetery awnings at Padobar

Memorial Gardens. On the third night, without a moon, that raff-
ish figure stalked up and down the newer plots with a pencil light
reading headstones and looking for fresh sprays of flowers.
Purring into the humid air, his soft curses awakened no Andrew
Russell.

TWENTY-SIX

"Crucified . . . *crucified!*" Skelote passed his forearm over a cluttered desk as if looking for a place to land. "You're sure about that cross business?"

Back through the open doorway came Janet's self-assured voice: "St. Andrew's cross, Lieutenant, I'm sure."

"Funny. Name was Andrew, too. Maybe we've got an educated killer here."

"Are you talking to me, Lieutenant?"

Skelote put his stubby fingers on his knees, pushed himself up an inch beyond his normal five-eleven slouch, and carried his two hundred twenty-odd pounds through the outer office to chip a cigarette butt at the sand trap in the hall. "Where's my call from the county sheriff's office?"

"I don't know, I'm not in the county sheriff's office." A single key struck the typewriter. She regarded him through thick lenses, frowning, then inserted a scrap of correction tape and murmured: "You're just ornery enough to shoot your alter ego, Lieutenant."

"That correction tape work on people?"

She was young, college-scented, and on top of her fine mind

he had to put up with her refusing to wear the dispatcher's uniform. Since the government paid her salary with CETA funds, she was not strictly on the force, she maintained.

Skelote pawed papers on his desk for a pen. There were at least nine hundred Bics hidden somewhere in and about the office. He had personally lost all of them in twenty-one years on the force, most used only once.

"If that Lieutenant Hobson manages to return my call, tell him I'm out to lunch and ask him to leave a time when I can get hold of him."

The water cooler chugged away as he passed outside between droopy state and national flags. He donned sunglasses, slid behind the wheel of the issued Plymouth, started up an engine that sneezed and then subsided to a whisper, and rolled off the lot. Glorious day. Seventy-seven, sunny. He had intended to drive to Orlando to see his granddaughter, little Brenda, two and a half. He remembered the last trip, two months ago, when she had appeared in the kitchen with a club foot composed of nine socks mounted one over the other—"See my new boot, Grampa?" Today it was supposed to be Disney World, but instead of little girl squeals it had begun with big girl screams.

Conspicuously there weren't any blacks on the streets this morning. Sheila Mason's hysteria was already spreading through the community. By night there wouldn't be any whites. Looks followed Skelote as he eased down to Shore's diner, questioning looks, despairing looks, accusative looks, suspicioning looks. No group could look at you as potently as a town full of octogenarians. He knew how to handle punks on motorcycles trying to look tough, or out-of-town speeders with do-you-know-who-I-am expressions, but little old ladies turning away from you could beat homicidal passion all to blazes after a while.

Inside the square front greasy spoon known as Shore's, he took a stool. The waitress, Arlene, ambled over without the formality of a menu in a room that was too high, too old, too empty. Knocking the counter and missing the sound his ring always made, Skelote piped, "Where's my bean soup?"

"Didn't your mother breast-feed you, Jack? It's no wonder you and Claudia split. Bean soup, bean soup, bean soup. She must have been a helluva cook."

Arlene had a voice like an alto sax with a bad reed, but Skelote loved her. He danced his fingers together while she opened the can, dumped it in a pan, and curdled it in less than a minute.

"What does alter ego mean?" he asked suddenly.

"It's not on the menu."

"I got one of those smart-ass college kids working for me. Say, give me four dollars' worth of that gum in the showcase. I'm trying to kick cancer."

She brought it back when he was finishing his soup. "No wonder they call you gumshoe."

He dropped his remaining cigarettes in the wire basket outside and put the survival kit in the glove compartment after unwrapping a stick. Gripping the wheel in both hands like the bar on a roller coaster, he backed out. Driving was not his best skill— "Jalopy Jack," downtowners called him because of the cratered, crumpled chrome that invariably graced his vehicles—but he compensated by turtling along at minimal speeds under the guise of cruising. Still, the car remained for him a malicious mystery. Like now, for instance. He had done nothing to make the beast cough and die like this, except . . . forget to put gas in it.

He coasted inconspicuously into a parking space, got out, sauntered around to the trunk, unlocked it, shook the empty gas can. Did he want to add another chapter to the legend of Jalopy

Jack or could this be done discreetly? A young towhead was lolling on a parking meter thirty feet away. Skelote chewed gum and regarded the sky. The alternative was Jalopy Jack syphoning gas in the police parking lot. He loosened his tie.

"Son." He tried to project this like a ventriloquist. "Want some gum, son?" The boy trudged over while Skelote unwrapped a stick of spearmint. "How old are you, son?"

"Eleven. Got any other flavors?"

"Spearmint's good for you. Keep you from smoking." The boy looked disinterested. "Here, take the whole pack. You look like a smart young businessman, how'd you like to earn fifty cents?"

"I'll get your gas for a buck."

Little felon belonged behind bars, Skelote reflected. "Tell you what, son, I'm almost down to plastic for cash, but I've got . . . two dollars and three cents here. Wanta count it?" To his disgust the boy did. "Now, all you have to do is pick up that two-gallon can there behind my car—*don't point*—and take it to the Great Eastern station in the next block. Fill it and bring it back. That'll leave you nearly a dollar in change. If you can put that gas in my tank and keep your lip buttoned, the change is yours."

He dumped the money into the boy's avaricious palms and retired to the doorway of a Christian bookstore. In due course the youngster returned, apparently able to handle the weight of the red can effortlessly, and gave a wave that snapped Skelote back into line. Skelote thought the container sounded half full as the gas was poured. When the boy was done, he sat the can down, waved, and trudged off.

Skelote tossed the can in the backseat, and considered checking the tank with a match. If it did hold any gas, it didn't show on the gauge. But the Plymouth sneezed to life, and he whispered across town to a distant Sunoco station.

Two teams of gangly seventh graders were pounding a basketball up and down the civic gym when he returned to the Mu-
nicipal Building. It sounded like pom-pom guns on Guam.

"We have a twenty-seven in progress at four-four-eight Wilson
Parkway," Janet was reading over the radio.

That was a prowler. Probably another utility lineman spotted
by a senior citizen. "The trouble with gum is you can't light it,"
Skelote said with annoyance. "What about my call?"

"On your desk. Boy, you smell like gas."

"It's the bean soup."

He picked up the phone, tapped out the sequence. Busy. The
sandwich frame picture of Brenda caught his eye. ("How do
anteaters get the ants off their tongues, Grampa?") He tapped out
the number again and Lieutenant Hobson clattered into his ear.

"Oh, yeah, Skylot, sorry I missed you before."

"Ske-LOT-ee, Lieutenant. Listen, we're checking things out
on this murder down here, so I'd appreciate a little breathing
room—"

"Are you aware what's going on county-wide, Skeelot?"

"I think so—"

"Our men actively investigate every lead."

"I realize that. I called *you*, didn't I? I'm just telling you we
don't need citizen hysteria. So, if you don't mind, we'll handle
Padobar as if it's an isolated case."

"You know we don't operate that way. That's inefficient, repet-
itive, and downright incompetent. We've got the manpower, the
data, the lab . . . what have you got, Skylot?"

"The case. Look, call me Jack. And try to understand, Hobson,
we may need your facilities but we've got our own manpower.
You keep your investigation out of Padobar, and I'll give you what
I've got. All I want is for the papers not to hear you say it's con-

nected with the other murders. I know, I know, it's obvious, and they'll jump all over the similarity, but officially I want to tell the community not to leap to conclusions. And that means that they don't see county enforcement nosing around town."

"All right. It's pointless and time consuming, but if you'll give me what you've got, I'll play along for now. When can we get together?"

"This afternoon. Three-thirty. I'll come your way."

Four murders. More violence than Marlo County had seen since the Seminole Indian wars. Slowly unwrapping another stick of spearmint, Skelote pondered the winter's other events for connections. There had been traffic fatalities from two separate head-on collisions, Ohio tourists in the one case plowing over the median and striking the camper of a Vero Beach couple, a truck jackknifing in the other, encountering a local car as it pitched into the opposite lane. Luke Sutter's suicide was more suspect. No note, and yet Sutter had gone grocery shopping the day it happened—forty-seven dollars' worth—and it was all there, neatly put away in the refrigerator and the cupboards. He must have decided very suddenly to kill himself. Of the half-dozen suicides Skelote had seen in his lifetime, this seemed the most spontaneous and cruel. Then there was old Adler thrown from his horse and dragged. They never did decide what had spooked the animal or why it had apparently gone round and round the enclosure a dozen times or more until Adler was beyond identification. It still seemed to Skelote that if the horse had shied, he would avoid circling over the spot where it happened. But the possibility of murder had never been seriously considered. And finally there was the gravel slide out near the phosphate mine. A strong, middle-aged man like Steve Laberdie found under a mere foot of gravel that somehow—no one had bothered much over the mechanics—knocked him out and pinned him. Gravel piles were porous. Laberdie had to have lain there a considerable time to suffocate. And the whiskey bottle. If Laberdie had sat atop the pile at a discreet moment for a little unobserved drinking, why hadn't the bottle been broken in the slide? Skelote wished to hell there had been an autopsy. Laberdie's blood alcohol might have settled it.

So. Sutter, Adler, Laberdie. Sticking out like one, two, three. Maybe Padobar was getting more than its share of violence in Marlo County, and maybe he had more of an investigation to pursue than anyone knew. He ought to call around, he thought. See what kind of accidents and suicides the other departments had. Maybe murder was the number one way of dying in Marlo County.

TWENTY-SEVEN

OTTO WEAVED FROM side to side, steering one-handed and queuing up a succession of snake line curls through the puddles. There was a scented mugginess in the air, in patches, as if the flora were breathing hard after the storm. Kurt edged alongside and for a while their wheels, in profile, made illusionary links and releases like magician's rings.

"Is Jimmy going to make you a studio artist?" Kurt flung across as they coasted.

"I don't think so. I'm not that good. He says I've got to notice details better, that I draw women's upper lips and men's lower lips big like they were all like that. He's got a lot of clever ideas. You can see a person's inner expression by looking at them upside down, did you know that? If you just look around the eyes and the mouth."

Kurt thought it was crazy, but his gaze was drawn to another anomaly: a man with a phosphorescent green nose standing in a garden fifty yards away. Sunlight falling straight through the transparent green visor of his bucket hat explained the phenomenon. Ahead, geriatric tricycles began to converge in a line.

"Let's take a trail," said Otto, braking suddenly into a cluster of sand pines.

They had to stand and pedal to keep themselves moving in the lightly packed soil. But not many yards in, earth and trees grew sturdier, darker.

"Oleander," Otto said, pointing. "Ute says they're poisonous."

Kurt saw the tall shrubs with white flowers bent by droopy seed pods that seemed to have frozen in the act of spewing out their hearts. Like Ute. Ute was poisonous. One touch and . . .

Otto created detours over carpets of pine needles or threaded through trees where sparseness permitted. Then came a metallic clink—twice—under Otto's wheels. He semicircled back. Kurt veered off and stopped. Neither spoke. Both dismounted. With a kind of boyish reverence they converged around something on the ground.

They were staring at an animal, half-eaten, half-bloated, the serene globes of its eyes smoky, the weathered staves of its skeleton sticking out like architectural ruins. Its black muzzle was only a syrupy fuzz on the butt of a bristly toothed bone. And the chain whose end Otto had passed over was wrapped around its neck.

"Your father did this," Kurt whispered.

Otto kept staring at the piece of death, realizing that it had to be one of the hounds, trying not to remember another piece of death below the overhang of a cathedral roof in Germany.

"You know he did this," Kurt persisted. "He's sick."

"No."

"Then why is he like he is? Why does everyone put up with him?"

"How should I know?"

"But you do. All the family knows, except me. I'm not stupid, Otto, tell me."

"I can't." The tension at the bridge of his nose made the skin as white as the parched bones at their feet.

"Tell me something else, then. When I was only six or seven, we went with your father on a pilgrimage. You're older than me, so you must remember better. We went to Chartres. He took us by the hand through the whole cathedral. I remember some of the stained glass but not what he said about it. And the crypt. He showed us a place . . . and we did something. What did we do, Otto?" Otto's face became a wall. "Did we go—did I go with you—because I couldn't be allowed around when my sister's second confirmation took place?"

"Children aren't permitted to see second confirmations."

"What about now, Otto? Am I old enough now?"

"That's up to Grandmamma."

Kurt remained pointedly over the hound. Family! No one trusted him. Not Ute. Not Grandmamma. Not even Otto. In anger and frustration he lashed out: "Did Hans really fall from a cathedral roof, Otto?"

The baleful look he got never really left Otto's eyes the rest of the afternoon, and the ride back was marked only by the buzz of gears continuing the interface like a pair of bumblebees at odds in the afternoon sun.

▪   ▪   ▪

ALL THE REST of the day Kurt worked absently. He had succeeded in alienating both his cousins, but it was Chartres that remained on his mind. Chartres with its Gallo-Roman substructures and its pagan well that seemed in his dim recollection to go down, down, down into the earth. The well was the final passage. What was at the bottom? The legend claimed it was a human sacrifice.

And suddenly he realized that he was staring out the window at the chapel, a chapel that had its own well in the form of an overgrown cistern. Why not take a look? It was outside where he could run away if Detlef spotted him.

He chose a moment just after dark when everyone was occupied elsewhere to enter the kitchen and take a flashlight out of the drawer by the sink. Already from his gable he had seen the bone-white moon full in the sky, but he would need the flashlight to reveal the bottom of the cistern. Tucking it into the waistband under his sweatshirt, he closed the drawer and went into the living room.

"Play some cards?" Otto asked as he was at the door.

"Let him be, Otto," Gerta said from her chair, having seen an introspection about her grandson and deduced his need for solitude.

"I didn't eat my butterscotch pudding," Kurt offered. "It's in the refrigerator."

"Thanks."

Intuition was driving him, Kurt thought as he stepped into the cool night. But intuition seemed to be what was walling him out of the family, so maybe he should use what he had. He was determined to open any door, examine any book, pry in any secret he could find.

An armadillo slid away at his approach through the orchard, and then he saw the raised hummock of the cistern. Such a rich spurt of vegetation covered it! He had anticipated that his penknife would serve if it needed clearing, but now he saw that the mass of creepers was tightly interwoven at the top. Glancing back at the house and gates, he risked a pulse from the flashlight. The tangle went down some three feet to a wooden hatch.

Smarting, he cut and plucked from the top while the severed tendrils remained nested for the most part, as if the body of the thing resisted his efforts with a will of its own. After a few moments of futile work he examined his hands and delivered a disgusted kick to the thorny web. To his surprise it shot out of the depression en masse, like a tumbleweed. It had only been jammed into the mouth of the cistern. Suspicions tingling, he fell to his knees, reaching far down the shaft to the wooden hatch. Its weight threatened to pull him in, but he pressed his right shoulder against the earthen walls and managed to tug it slightly off center.

What came up instantly was an effluvial rot that drove him out of the depression. Something dead. Something newly dead. Holding his breath he crouched again, angling the flashlight into the dark ellipse. The light might as well have fallen on black velvet. But more of the interior was wafted to him, and this time he thought there was a trace of lime struggling with the putrescence. He lay flat on his stomach now, thrusting the flashlight into the opening. Glare and shadow refused to compromise except to reveal snatches of a surface perhaps twenty feet below. And then the flashlight slipped from his sweaty fingers and plummeted down, its yellow cone ripening as it shrank to expose, in a final burst of clarity, a moist glittering swell dappled as though with powdered sugar. The instrument nosed silently into that substance, leaving a cryptic red fairy ring around its translucent plastic cap.

Kurt straightened and wiped the sting from his eyes, and that was when he became aware of the car just prowling past the Chapel Lane gate. Panic touched his heart. He scrambled up and into the first line of trees as the silhouette prescribed a slow arc and began backing toward him. Then the brake lights brightened once and went off. A man got out before the chapel.

The soft diffusion from the car swept up Detlef's features, highlighting his hawkish stare and melting away years. Kurt remembered a very much older-looking Detlef who had stood behind the green Dodge surveying everything that first day, and it seemed he wasn't a hawk after all but a phoenix.

His uncle unlocked the trunk and took out a post-hole digger. Then fumbling for another key, he carried the tool toward the cellar side of the chapel.

Kurt wasted no time dashing to the lip of the exposed cistern. He was startled by a rhinoceros beetle crawling along the rim, and nausea at the foul smell nearly overcame him, but the hatch grated on while he gritted his teeth. Then he kicked the brier back into place, treading it down, and ran lightly through the orchard, across the drive, and behind the shed. Already he could hear the car coming. Circling to the far end of the house, he waited for his uncle to pull in the garage before he skipped spryly onto the porch.

"Well," Gerta greeted as he cushioned the screen door, "back so soon?"

"I changed my mind about cards," he blurted, dropping to his knees.

Astonished, Otto moved the butterscotch-smeared dessert glass aside and picked up the hand Kurt was dealing. Then the door opened. Kurt felt cause and effect being weighed around the room.

"Your play," he said, endeavoring to breathe normally.

"Why, Kurt, what happened to your hands?" Anna cried suddenly.

He turned his hands in careless examination of the bloody thorn marks, aware of his uncle's keener interest.

"Stray cat," he mumbled, satisfying no one. Looks were being composed behind him, but he stubbornly continued to play until that radiance that was his uncle passed from over his shoulder into the kitchen.

"Better put some Merthiolate on those scratches," Gerta said softly then.

He went upstairs to the bathroom and did the required painting with the plastic applicator. And as he gazed at the first scarlet stain, he recalled with a sickening tremor the flashlight embering into the stuff at the bottom of the cistern, and he prayed to God that the batteries would burn out before his uncle looked.

TWENTY-EIGHT

"PATHOLOGY," THE TECH answered the phone in a voice that seemed to take something for granted: *You have reached the slab lab. Let's have it. Don't waste the forensic pathologist's time. Who or what do you want sliced up now?*

But it wasn't a police agency calling with another body, or even an equipment supply house, or a research lab. It was just a person, an unaffiliated person, solo, public.

"I'm trying to find my brother-in-law," he said. "His name was Andrew Russell."

"I'm sorry, but we're just the lab. You'll have to talk to a local police agency or the sheriff's department for information about bodies."

"I was told he was there."

"He may have been, but we don't have anything to do with whether or not they come here or where they go afterward."

"You're saying he's not there now?"

The caller didn't sound indignant or outraged or hysterical or even grief-stricken, she thought. He sounded calm. "No, he's not here now."

179

"Then the autopsy is over."

"The autopsy was concluded a number of days ago."

"And he's been buried?"

Hesitation. A few of them were very cool, these disenfranchised relatives who crawled out of the woodwork, but in the end they talked to some neighborhood legal expert and got all jacked out of shape over the handling of their "loved one" and came after a bundle they could spend on solace. The legal thing was generally nothing to worry about, if the lab kept to its policies, but it was a hassle.

"I don't think he was buried," she said.

"I see. Well, what arrangements were made?"

"I'm not supposed to give out that information. We just follow instructions. If you want to check with the police agency involved, which would be the Padobar police, they can verify your interest in the deceased and any estate."

"I think you are protecting yourself, am I right? Well, I don't hold you responsible for anything. I simply want to know the whereabouts of my brother-in-law. I have letters to write, and I would like for those who knew him to not feel that he simply vanished from the face of the earth. Whatever happened is at an end. But where is the end?"

He had a quaint manner of speaking, but he sounded reasonable, she thought. He could find out anyway, why should she throw up roadblocks?

"He carried a donor card," she said. "His body went to science."

"Oh. Organ transplants and the like. What did they do with the rest of him?"

"Actually, I don't think his organs were transplantable after the autopsy and the delay, sir. He would have gone to a medical school for study."

"Ahh-h. A medical school. He would have liked that. Which medical school?"

Well, she had gone this far. "Just a minute, I'll check."

She didn't know why she said that. She remembered which school. It was the Cyril Institute. St. Petersburg. She drew a pair of lips on the notepad by the phone, then picked up the receiver and gave the stranger the information.

"*Saint* Petersburg," he repeated. "Well, well, well." Then he thanked her and hung up.

It occurred to her then that she hadn't asked his name.

■   ■   ■

BY COINCIDENCE THEY were showing an old print of *The Body Snatchers* with Boris Karloff at the Student Union the night of the break-in. The intruder got in through the roof, mounting with simian ease and forcing a flimsy casement on a dormer. Energy conservation was a priority that year and all the corridors were dark except for the red shimmer of exit signs along rippled linoleum. Level by level he descended, looking for the obvious signs: large containers, a chilled room, the smell of formaldehyde. He found all three in the basement.

The formaldehyde and the chill were evident before he located the light switch, and then the flutter of fluorescent tubes revealed the tank at the far end. It was sunk into the floor, almost level, covered by stainless-steel doors on a gasket. They were locked, but the simple mechanism was not meant to withstand anything more than pranksters who wished to place the dean in effigy or an opponent's football helmet in the tank without doing any real damage. A single hard pull bent one door lip and disengaged the lock bar.

There were four bodies hanging by their ears in the green tile depths. Smarting from the fumes, the intruder straddled the edge and hauled up on the first headpiece. It came at him with a rush and a grin. The mouth had been cut away and also the brows, giving a lunatic gaiety to the lipless teeth and lidless eyes. The skull was shaven; a wedge had been taken out of the left hemisphere, like a piece of marble cake. From the head alone he would not have been able to tell it was a woman, but there were breasts, misshapen and stiff, like huge drops of tallow congealed on a yellow-green candle, and he let the corpse plunge back into its bath.

The next one was heavier. He only managed the shoulders free before he saw that it was an obese male, younger than Andrew Russell. The fat man had drowned trying to rescue a little boy off Clearwater, and his great body sluiced back into place as if resuming the search.

Bracing again, the intruder yanked up hard on the third assembly. This one shot completely out of the tank. It had been severed below the rib cage, an elderly male, eyes and mouth closed, a little tension at the bridge of the nose. There was admonition in the face, as if it were mildly censuring all this desecration of the temple of the body that it had undergone. The intruder lowered it gently, thinking now that the cadavers were probably arranged by the length of time they had been here. Andrew Russell would be the freshest—the fourth one, the one on the end.

He hauled it up and to the side, a tuberous thing that had once been a man, as inflexible and appendaged as a mandrake root now. Its chest flopped open like a vest, its face seemed to be plunging after its entrails. But the marks on the wrists and ankles were the marks of a crucifixion.

Andrew Russell.

No mistake about it.

Unbuttoning his shirt, the intruder pulled a canvas bag from around his torso. From his waistband he withdrew a small, sharp hatchet. Then he began stuffing the body head first into the canvas bag, working efficiently and swiftly to dismember what hung out.

When it was all arranged as tightly as cordwood, he cleaned up the scraps and smears with a rag and tossed that in the bag also. Then he hefted the bundle onto his shoulders and rolling like a sailor over heavy seas made his way up to the first-floor level.

He had to go to three exists before he found one that wasn't chained from the inside, but on the second he had given the roll-bar handle a kick out of frustration. The noise was picked up on the security monitor—a small microphone affixed to the ceiling above the entrance—and duly carried to campus security four blocks away. The honors student on duty that night had gone to the pay phone to get help on a calculus problem from his girlfriend and didn't hear the telltale sounds until the intruder was hacking away with the hatchet on a small padlock at the third exit.

"God, Sherry, oh, God!" he exclaimed and ran for the intercampus phone at his desk. From the dangling receiver he had left behind in the pay phone carrel, his girlfriend's voice responded to the declaration of alarm: "Oh, come on, Johnny, the problems aren't that difficult!"

By the time he alerted the police, the intruder was halfway through the hasp lock and had the dead bolt back. The sergeant in the station who took the call then had to convey it to the dispatcher, who put out a patrol car alert. The unit closest to the Cyril Institute was handling a family confrontation half a mile north of the Anatomy Building. There were a dozen bystanders in the hall of a tenement, because the old man was drunk and the old lady had a knife and three terrified children were backed against a wall listening to the threats, so nobody paid any attention to the dispatcher crackling out of the Dick Tracy thing on the tall policeman's hip. The next nearest unit had to come across St. Pete from the Gulf side, and they were nearly broadsided at midtown.

"Fuck the call," one of them—the passenger—said to the other, "I'm retiring in two weeks!"

So the younger one grudgingly slowed down, and by the time they reached the break-in scene the intruder and his terrible baggage were home free. The cruiser actually passed the body thief as he was slamming the trunk of his car on the canvas bag a block from the Anatomy Building.

▪   ▪   ▪

DEAN BORKOWSKI CAME hurtling along the boulevard outside the Student Union in his Lincoln Continental just as *The Body Snatchers* was letting out. He had to hit the brakes to avoid a half-dozen students who were clowning on the curb. One of them flopped ghoulishly over the hood of his car. The youth rolled in agony and pressed his face to the windshield while he crossed his eyes. They were hazel, the dean noticed in the glare of a streetlight, and they straightened out in a hurry when he opened the car door a crack, causing the dome light to fall over his own features.

"Dennis . . . Dennis Watts, is that you?"

Dennis Watts slid off the hood like brand "B" tomato ketchup and disappeared around the wheel well. For all the dean knew, the sophomoric sophomore could have been in it as he hit the accelerator. He also hit the pulse wipe on the windshield washer to clean off Dennis Watts's lip prints. There were two police cars at the Anatomy Building when the dean parked in the fire lane out front. He hurried over to one of the drivers and identified himself.

"Looks like our break-in came out of that door over there," said the officer at the wheel, pointing to the maintenance entrance. "The inside padlock is smashed. We haven't figured out how he got in yet. How do you get in, Professor?"

The dean detected something colloquial and mocking in the erroneous address "Professor." "Through a side door with a double lock," he said. "We have a great deal of valuable equipment in there—a great deal. One of the microscopes alone is insured for a hundred thousand dollars. And the slides are irreplaceable."

"They have a value on the open market?"

"I don't know. I suppose . . . somewhere. The officer who called me said you hadn't found anything missing yet."

"That was me, and I said 'vandalized.' We hadn't found any vandalism. Can't tell what's missing."

"Hadn't? Did you say you 'hadn't' found any vandalism?"

"Since then we've visited the basement. Someone forced a door cover on a tank of some chemical, looks like."

"Oh, my God, those smart-ass kids," said Dean Borkowski. "Every time they show that damn movie . . ."

Dean Borkowski expected to find a Boy Scout neckerchief on one of the bodies when they reached the basement, or another spurious suicide note from his wife's ostensible lover there in the tank, but he didn't expect to come up one cadaver short.

"The little bastards have gone too far this time," he fumed. "Have you any idea how hard it is to get a suitable specimen for study? I suppose we'll find it in the lobby of the girls' dormitory or the like, but by then its condition will surely have deteriorated."

"Well, let us know if you come up with any specific suspects," said the policeman when the report was done.

Thereafter, the dean carried an image around in his mind of a corpse that day by day moldered. He saw its spongy canescence go to desert yellow and its mushy exterior wither. He pictured the nose eroding, the eye sockets deepening, and all the cross sections melting into one another like a parfait beyond its hour. It occurred to him later, when recovery hopes were all but gone, that the crucified corpse might turn up on Easter morning, a gross joke by some young atheist, but he didn't suggest this to the police.

St. Petersburg's finest were busy enough with the living. No one bothered about the background of the corpse. No one thought the theft significant. No one contacted Jack Skelote of the Padobar department or talked to a petite blonde at the Marlo County pathology lab. The closest anyone came to the truth was that moment when Dean Borkowski mused about a resurrection of the crucified corpse on Easter morn.

Resurrection, in a sense, was what it was all about.

TWENTY-NINE

BALMY SPRING CURRENTS at just the right temperature pulled chemical triggers right and left, the Muscovy ducks began making love in public, and the motels dropped their seasonal rates, but in the five municipalities of north Marlo County, it rained blood. In Padobar, Jack Skelote got wet.

He was driving to work when he heard about the second crucifixion. Details were sketchy over the car radio. Unidentified white male found in the backyard outside his home in Trinity nailed to a cross.

Skelote crammed three sticks of spearmint into his mouth.

It took him two hours to get hold of Chief Wiggins, Trinity P.D., and then he couldn't find a pen to write down the details. Phil Gibbs, dead of shock and loss of blood, had been spiked to a Latin cross—"a reg'lar Christian kind," characterized Wiggins. He had been discovered at dawn by a consortium of neighborhood dogs. Skelote promised a duco of his own file in exchange for a copy of the autopsy when it came in.

He was particularly anxious about that. The autopsy. The report on Andrew Russell, now lost in the paper sediments on his desk, mentioned needle marks on the right forearm. If he had been diabetic, or on drugs, there would have been similar tracks on the left arm, since he was right-handed. And his blood had been normal. Skelote initially wondered if false starts of the spikes could have been responsible, but the report was specific—needle marks. An impeccable church service record seemed to have been Andrew Russell's only passion. Was that connected?

In a way, it was, though Skelote had no way of knowing that yet. Lieutenant Hobson could have simplified things, if he had sent the files he had promised, but the documents languished despite Skelote's calls until they were finally delivered two days after the Trinity murder. By then Skelote had already seen the autopsy report on Phil Gibbs. Among the details: needle marks.

The autopsies of the man run through with a spear and of the victim whose brains had been dashed out proved similar in that regard. Only the beheading case made no mention of marks. Skelote pondered it in the torpor of his office, and over a bowl of Arlene's bean soup, and while chewing gum to the pom-poming of basketballs in the civic gym. The answer was simple. If nothing was going into the bodies, then something was coming out.

Like blood.

The reason the beheading victim hadn't been tapped was because the murderer got all the blood he needed without an extraction.

Skelote called the medical examiner's office and got hold of a certain petite blonde.

"Oh, Lieutenant," she said after he had asked for the examiner, "did that man who was looking for his brother-in-law ever get hold of you?"

"What man?"

"I never got his name. He said he was Andrew Russell's brother-in-law."

Skelote began to tingle. "What did he look like?"

"I only talked to him over the phone. He wanted to know where his brother-in-law was, and I said that you could tell him about that and the estate and everything."

"The 'estate' went to taxes and his church. He didn't have any living relatives."

"Oh," she said. "Oh, shit."

"He never got hold of me. That should tell you something."

"I gave him the information he wanted."

"What?"

"I told him where Russell was."

"Refresh me."

"Cyril's Institute, St. Petersburg."

" 'Oh, shit,' is right. Somebody ought to bury him quick. As long as he's above ground, some reporter will make an issue out of him. That's probably what happened. Some reporter got to you with a tall one."

"Sorry. But what can he do about it except hassle them?"

"It's a ghoul of a reporter probably. They're starting to phone in from all over the country." He had actually been awakened that morning by an early news show host for a TV station in Newark wanting to know some juicy details over the air. Skelote had given him some juicy language to go with the juicy details and after the fifth tape delay beep-out, the host thanked him and hung up. "Some graveyard hack in Detroit probably pruned you for an angle he's got on a scum piece for a scandal sheet."

"I don't think so," the blonde replied a little frostily.

"Yeah? What's your theory?"

"My theory is you overlooked a sister of Andrew Russell's."

"No doubt. Quintets probably. Well, give me the slab master."

She gave him silence, and then the examiner was on the line and Skelote asked his question: "Would it be possible to get blood from the arms of a fresh cadaver?"

"Possible. Easier from the heart."

"How much?"

"Just what remained in the capillaries and veins."

"Would it take a lot of . . . you know, tries with the needle?"

"Depends on whether the person knew what they were doing, and how much they wanted."

"Thanks."

Skelote had another thought after he hung up. Maybe the crucified men had been bled before death. That would help explain the relatively short durations—according to lab estimates—of their agony before expiration. Loss of blood had been an unreliable factor. Age and condition were assumed to have made the difference. He opened a bottom drawer to rest his feet. Now, what the hell did it all mean?

That the whole thing was racial still seemed likely. The use of crosses might be a backlash aimed at the KKK. They might even be dealing with a Klan-type organization. One man spiking victims to cumbersome crosses and erecting them was no mean feat. Familiarity with his prey was almost a certainty with the killer, yet the geographical range, like the methods, was so varied. Those things seemed to coincide with a terrorist motive. But Skelote could not rid himself of the notion that the gravel slide, the hanging, and the accident with the horse might also be added to the toll. If so, the very subtlety of their perpetration contradicted terrorism as a motive. Those "accidents" had all preceded the known pattern. Maybe emboldened by success, the murderer had broadened his plan to overt terrorism. Profile: a lone, deranged, black sadist, very strong, very clever. Or a group.

He toyed with the idea of having Laberdie exhumed. Needle marks would answer some questions, if the body wasn't too decomposed. But he ended up calling a psychologist he sometimes played tennis with and arranged a match for Saturday morning.

On Friday, Norse Chapel discovered the third crucifixion.

On Saturday, Skelote appeared at the scruffy pair of city courts wearing a scruffy pair of shorts, a scruffy pair of tennis shoes, and the look of a man adrift in a storm. It was early. His sleepy body demanded oxygen from the mere effort of waking, dressing, eating, walking from the car. Drugged by the perfumed air, he spread his arms over the court-side bench and listened to the mournful tri-note of the swings down toward the lake.

Minutes later a mint blue Volare bumped along the access road beyond the old fence patched with chicken wire. Out stepped a medium man—height, weight, build—with calves like inverted bowling pins. Crisp and scented, he reminded Skelote of a line of yachting pennants, nautical white overlaid with flashy blues and reds. He carried an enormous, imitation leather tote bag that sported two racket handles like drumsticks on a brass turkey. Twin wristbands implied that he would use both at once: two-gun Herschel Kalb.

"Hello, Jack."

"Morning, Herschel."

The tote bag boomed down, and they sat silently for a few seconds in the limp air.

"Looks like we beat the rush," Kalb said then. "Nice day."

"New pair of shoes, I see."

Herschel crossed one leg, revealing the snowy peg molars of one sole. "Yeah. Arthur Ashe. New racket, too." He unsheathed

Excalibur, turning its flat gray blade for examination. "Head Competition. Victor Imperial gut. Sixty pounds."

Skelote hefted it, tried to push the strings. "Fiberglass and aluminum. It'll warp. Don't leave it in a hot trunk or you'll wind up swinging a pretzel."

"That was the old model. This is a Competition two. More boron in it."

Herschel stood, flexed his knees. He had on mid-calf white socks and an elbow strap. A floppy Australian-style hat surfaced from the depths of the tote, which he carefully adjusted over his thick coppery hair. Next came the sprays—one for the grip, one for the strings.

Skelote took off his watch and retrieved a can of skinned Wilson tennis balls (opened the month before) from alongside the net. Herschel reached for his own as Skelote had expected. "These will do." He raised a can of Pen's capped by a plastic pressurizer. Dropping them to assay the bounce, he then checked the net height with his racket—a length and a width, like a cross, Skelote couldn't help thinking—and skipped back to the baseline. Skelote dropped the Wilson's and ambled to his own end.

"Playing much?" Herschel inquired with veiled anxiety.

Skelote grunted as he pushed the first shot back. "Don't you read the papers?"

"You sure as hell . . . play more than me." Two more exchanges ensued before he added: "Played once since the last time with you."

Skelote smiled at the lie. "Rough or smooth?" He spun the racket and peered closely at the hatching above the throat.

"Smooth."

"Rough. You serve. I'll take this side."

Herschel bent over twice, raised his knees in a little jig. "I'll take a couple," he shouted and executed the first of two pirouettes that began softly and ended in lunges. He netted both practice serves. "Okay. Play these."

Skelote braced for mock war. The first serve followed the practice ones into the net. The second contained all the fierce windup of the first, but pinged absurdly off the racket. Skelote trotted in, stiffened to a halt, and pummeled the thing out of the court.

"Fifteen love," Herschel announced.

The first game went to the server on the second advantage. They changed ends and Skelote found himself vexed by his opponent's delay to employ a little yellow towel, more spray, and a different dance in the receiver's court. Herschel Kalb, with his waxy freckled skin, his floppy hat over Harpo Marx hair, his little bowlegged flex, was a frog capped by a mushroom. Skelote lost his own serve, too.

They played an hour and a half before yielding to dehydration and the pressure of other players waiting in boredom for death or defeat to end the match. Sweating and friendly, they retired to the park, discussing shots, confessing weaknesses, commiserating.

"Next time we use my Wilson's," Skelote, who had lost in split sets, concluded. He gulped water from the fountain.

"Your gum's melted." Herschel handed him the pack he had scooped up in clearing the court.

"Shit." Skelote waved toward a picnic table. "Let's sit down awhile." He could feel the clinical Herschel Kalb's peering eyes trying to read his purpose. "I assume you've followed the news accounts of the murders. You have any notions about what's behind it?"

"Oh, I could speculate."

"Speculate, damn it."

"Too little data for anything meaningful."

"What do you think police work is? When I come to you with a court case, I'll have data and you won't have to guess. Right now I want to know where to look for evidence."

"All right, all right . . . let me see if I've got the background. The first was that decapitation in Cicadia—"

"It's possible there were others. Off the record. But go on."

"The second," Herschel continued carefully, "was a clubbing of some kind. And the third, a spear. Then there were two crucifixions—"

"Three. Norse Chapel yesterday. A minister . . . upside down on a cross made out of railroad ties. The whole cross was inverted outside his church."

"My God. All right, three. All violent, all different, all white men. It could be racial. Or it could be a personality disorder."

"A sociopath?"

"Well, we don't use that word anymore. Let's say he might manifest antisocial behavior."

Skelote mistrusted psychology, but he felt that no matter how badly the Herschel Kalbs bandied terms and labels, they did have a nice collection of personality models. And that was precisely what he wanted: a few coats to try on his murderer. If none of them fit, at least he might get some useful measurements.

"Give me a for instance," he said.

"A for instance would be . . . someone with an overbearing mother, let's say—or the other extreme—and a father who was missing or had abandoned his role."

"Wait a minute. What's the other extreme? Overbearing and what?"

"Not caring."

"Oh." Skelote slipped his watch on.

"It might be the way he handles resentment, for instance."

"You mean this guy is killing his father?"

"It's possible he could be dumping resentment by killing, getting even, picking victims who remind him of his father."

"Then he's white, like the victims."

"That would follow, of course. He'd be what we call a four-eight on the MMPI, very high on the four."

"And what, pray tell, is that?"

"An MMPI? Minnesota Multi-phasic Personality Inventory. That's a test with a series of scales—nine, I think, plus three validity scales."

"Validity?"

"Catch questions to see if he's faking. The other scales give a profile of his personality, like a four would be PD—personality disorder. Eight—I think it's eight—is the SC, schizophrenia. He'd probably be a high four-eight. On the eight he might show just a keep-to-himself type. I'll have to check the cookbook, I'm not sure of the numbers."

"That's all right." Skelote resisted the flow toward academics. "I just want a word picture of a murderer. Would this guy likely have a record?"

"He might. If he failed to internalize social values, he might have a juvenile record. That's one of the clinical yardsticks we—"

"What about the crosses? Could he be religious?"

"He could. There's a connection on the eight, the schizophrenic scale."

"But it's not likely?"

"No, I didn't say that. Do your murders show anything else religious?"

Skelote seemed not to hear the question. "So . . . my strong suits are 'antisocial' and 'withdrawn.' That's if he isn't a group. Not a hell of a lot, is it?" He stood up, lifting the hem of his shirt for ventilation. "Well, thanks for your help, Herschel, but between you and me, I think I'll lean on the racial angle awhile."

"I told you it was just a guess."

Moving with less spring than when he had arrived, Herschel Kalb hauled his paraphernalia back to the mint blue Volare and eased down the access road. Skelote returned to his own car after another long drink at the fountain, but sat watching the brisk play on the far court until a siren intruded. It was the rescue truck, followed by a patrol car, light flashing. He thought nothing, said nothing, just swung quickly behind the wheel of his Plymouth. He caught them at the gate of the Hauptmann studio on a turnoff called Chapel Lane.

■　　■　　■

BILL MACKEY SPOKE a few words to the driver of the rescue truck while pumping his stiffened fingers in the direction of the chapel. Then he jumped back and they went streaming in. A knot of people stood outside the side entrance of the chapel. From the orchard came relentless animal roaring.

Detlef's voice, low with restrained power, called the rescuers down the cellar steps. For just a second Skelote came face-to-face with him, absorbing his lethal glance. Then they crowded in and seemed to freeze, oblivious to the smell of propane gas and feces. There was no rush. It was too late. One of the rescue men cleared his throat discreetly.

"Do you want it left this way, Lieutenant?"

Skelote pawed his sweaty face as if to change expressions. "How did it happen?"

"I'm the studio master," Detlef introduced himself wearily. "He came down here without permission. The hounds were loose, and I couldn't get here in time." He presented his own raked arm within a torn sleeve. "I chained the hounds in the orchard after-ward."

"Didn't he know the dogs were here?"

"He knew. But he might have thought they were chained."

"Where were you when it started?"

"In the chapel. He was probably looking for me. To come see his sketches."

Skelote sighed heavily, turned his back on the carnage. "Clean it up."

One of the rescue crew went for a body bag. Skelote trudged up the stone steps feeling nauseated but optimistic that this was not another atrocity by a madman. The horrible rending in the cellar was an obvious departure from the pattern, traceable, partially witnessed. The dogs would have to be destroyed, of course.

Sunlight struck him as though he had been entombed for a long time as he walked around the chapel. How long would it take for the studio master to run from inside to the cellar, he won-dered. The victim looked like he'd spent a month with an alliga-tor. Could the dogs have done that in a minute or two? He tried the chapel door. It didn't budge. It had that immovable feel of a solid door and a solid lock. "A mighty fortress is our God," said the verse carved into the lintel. Maybe the floors were a foot thick. Maybe the studio master took a little time figuring out all the commotion. He'd ask for the key later, he decided, and went over to Sergeant Carruthers on the edge of the orchard.

"Man's best friend," Carruthers said, gesturing toward two dogs. The beasts were still in a carnal lather: jaws salivating, eyes afire, claws spread and tearing up the earth at the ends of their tethers. They hadn't gotten that way naturally. Someone had *over-*trained them to be watchdogs.

"Probably brought them from a redneck with a house full of guns and German army helmets," Skelote said.

"Mighty hard for dogs like that to transfer loyalty."

"Amen. The guy who chained them out here got his arm laid open." Skelote decided he didn't need to check the chapel, after all. Tarzan couldn't have broken these dogs loose from a kill they hadn't finished, and a school of piranhas couldn't have done it any faster. "Make sure you get a statement from the studio master, Carruthers."

Bill Mackey, white and grim, was consoling a group of women, all of whom Skelote recognized as he approached, feeling like a tidal wave in a flood. A little apart stood two young men.

"Excuse me, ladies. I'm out of uniform, but—"

"I know you, Lieutenant."

"Yes, frau, I guess we've seen each other enough over the years. I'm sorry we couldn't have been formally introduced under better circumstances."

Gerta nodded, puckering. "What can we do to expedite your business, Lieutenant?"

"Well, some routine questions need answering. But I can come back another time."

"That would be most gracious of you."

"One thing, though. I don't know the name of the victim yet."

There was a respectful pause for the emergence of the body bag carried between attendants.

"His name was James Ignatius Pelt," Gerta said.

THIRTY

THEY HAD BEEN wincing in the sun outside that terrible cellar, and now they sat coolly shadowed in the living room. Ute was the first to speak her mind: "Why did you let him bring them here, Mama?" The hounds, she meant.

If Anna heard, she didn't have an answer. She sat braced in her rocker, as if it were hurtling through space.

"He was teaching me to sketch," Otto murmured, staring at the floor.

Kurt sat against the wall, the flat plane of his face looking darker than usual, because violence and death seemed to be reeling all around him. He hated this place. He hated what they were, a sinister little group with murky secrets.

"Why did he go to the cellar?" Otto asked distantly.

"I don't know, child," croaked Gerta.

The use of the word "child" aggravated Otto as much as it did Kurt, and he was suddenly persistent. "What made him go down there? What did he want? He wouldn't have gone there without being asked?"

"It was Uncle Detlef's fault," Ute sparked.

"Was it?" The words rustled out of Gerta's withered throat as if snatched. "How I envy you. You with your wise eyes that see only before and after a thing. My eyes saw only my son with his shirt torn and his arm opened to the bone. My ears told me that the hounds were attacking him while he tried to save Jimmy in the cellar. My heart told me that he felt compassion for us when he kept us back afterward. And now we wait for him while he does what must be done."

The young people smoldered silently, but Ute's kitten seemed to ground them by brushing from leg to leg and jumping into Gerta's lap. What she said was true. They knew it was true.

"Have you brought an olive branch from your mistress?" the old matriarch cooed to the kitten. "Grandmamma doesn't like to scold her family. But—"

There was a shotgun report from the orchard. And another. Recoils punched into the room like the gaveling of a death sentence.

"What happened today is finished," Gerta said then. "But we're closing the studio for the time being. Bill Mackey will be paid, and after the funeral it will remain closed for an indefinite period."

Anna still sat frozen. Since that horrible moment when the lumpy body bag had surfaced from the cellar, conversation seemed to her like a recorded thing—foregone, unengageable.

"Jimmy spoke of a sister to me once," Gerta said. She rocked and the cadence seemed to reinforce their bonds like a lullaby. "I don't suppose he ever mentioned where she lived to any of you?"

And then they heard Detlef's steps striding purposefully along the drive. Kurt was struck by the optical effect of his uncle's coming into view: first, the pale shade through gauzy curtains of a dissipated man as he had been the day he arrived; then an enlarged and clarified Detlef coming onto the porch behind the screen, minutely graphed on the grid of fine wire like a blueprint; and finally the metamorphosed man entering the room, fresher, more vital than Kurt had ever seen him before. The bland smell of gunpowder and scorched oil reached them together with Detlef's glittering scrutiny. Martin's twelve-gauge hung broken down over his arm.

"You should have the bodies examined for rabies," Gerta declared. "Did they both scratch you?"

"I've already disposed of them."

"They could have contracted it, you know. Outside, at night."

"Worry about Kurt. He was scratched by a stray cat. That could be far more dangerous."

Kurt glanced at his hands where the brier scratches from his intrusion were still healing, and the bottom seemed to drop out of his stomach. His uncle knew. He had thrown something in the cistern and saw the flashlight, and now he knew. Whatever sanctuary there was in being family, Kurt's safety was in serious doubt, because the power was shifting. Who was in charge now?

Late that night, when the shutters on the chapel were outlined in red and yellow light from the renovations in progress within, he slipped his bathrobe on and padded downstairs. The breeze was steady through the screens. He could hear the kitten mewing outside, free for the first time in the compound. There was a glimmer under Gerta's door. He tapped lightly.

"Come in," she crooned.

He stepped in, suddenly uncertain as to what he would say.

"I've been expecting you. Close the door and come over to my side."

He crossed over, accepting a place on the edge of the mattress. Her femininity seemed somehow grotesque in the pink silk of a nightgown.

"You've carried this trouble of yours long enough, child. Now you must tell me what it is and see if we two can solve it."

He forsook her gaze for a row of easier eyes in the photos on the walls.

"I just don't fit here," he said.

"You're homesick."

"No. I didn't fit there either, after father died."

The old white head drooped. "That is quite normal, you know." She formed her lips into a moue. "Where is it you think you do belong?"

He shrugged.

"Does a spring river fit its banks? You're growing, changing, why shouldn't you be restless? When you've reached your crest you'll settle into a course, Kurt. And it will fit you. It may be here, it may be somewhere else. You'll know, and you'll belong because you want to."

"But I want to belong here. Otto and Ute belong. Why am I so different?"

Her dry fingers moved over his. "The only difference is how you feel," she said.

He inhaled, finding it painful to be specific. "What about second confirmation?"

"An event. Not a state of being. You'll go through it."

"When? Ute said it would change me. Maybe that's why I don't fit now. And what about the *gift*?"

The wrinkles of Gerta's face aligned themselves in a merry cascade.

"If any of us understood the mechanics of that, we'd gladly pass it around. Not every Hauptmann has had it. Some didn't even know they had it, or how to use it, until after second confirmation." Her voice began to crackle like tinder igniting. "Survival, contrary to what you may have been taught, is not the skip of civilization from one great mountaintop to the next. What touched us . . . what touched us most from century to century wasn't war, or famine, or plague, it was persecution. What we believe in has remained unchanged since the beginning. We are the rock. The world turns truth inside out, and there is nothing . . . *nothing* in mankind's album that doesn't have its mirror image. If we cling to our ways, we will survive. The gift is no more than an echo of mental acuities that were sharpest at times of persecution. It enabled us to recognize our enemies by sensing what they feared, or didn't fear."

He had never heard her speak this way before; and it seemed, by her tone, that she was clearing up mysteries for him, but all the time it got murkier. Still, he wanted to say the right thing, to fashion a key out of words.

"I read some of the things in the attic," he confessed cautiously. "Those things that were believed by all those sects . . . those aren't our beliefs, are they?"

He sounded like a little boy now, asking with hope, pleading to keep his innocence intact. She understood. It was an old ritual in the family. The young learning from their elders. Perhaps not quite this way, but the way would always change with the times even though the path must still be offered.

"What you saw in those books were prisms, each reflecting its ray of light from a single illuminating source. We believe in that source."

"How could they come from the same source? They contradicted each other."

"Because they were fragmented, because they held only a grain apiece. Do you know what happens when you mix all the colors, every possible hue and tint? Did Jimmy ever tell you what you get?"

He swallowed dryly at the studio artist's name. "You get black."

"You get white, pure white. That's the way it was in the beginning. When the whiteness was broken down it yielded colors which seemed unlike on the surface. It's as if a thousand people each lit a candle from the first fire and bore it off into the future where they began arguing about which one held the true fire. They forgot the source and their own kinship. But if all the candles were brought back together again, they would make a single flame."

She did not intend to tell him what was at the heart of the family, he realized. All the little parables and analogies were just so much scrollwork to mislead the eye. "Forgive me, Grandmamma, but I don't see how that relates to what I'm asking."

"I've given you the framework already. You could reason it out. The details, however, are disconcerting. Without sufficient wisdom, foresight, and contemplation, you would never understand. Second confirmation—when you're ready—will give you the time, the atmosphere, and the details to see it."

"What about Uncle Detlef? What made him worthy of second confirmation?"

"Cruelty is not always what it seems," she replied coldly. "Detlef occupies an unusual position in the family hierarchy, but he isn't without precedent. Criticizing him won't make you any wiser, young man. There have been many more generations of contrition and service than tainted ones. Despite your impression, your uncle does believe in God. Fervently. He feels Him more than you and I." Her hands twitched on the blanket. "And now, I've answered your questions as best I can for the moment. I'm saddened from a long, dreary day, and your youthful impertinence wearies me ..."

"I didn't mean to be impertinent." His voice was sanded smooth as he rose off the bed.

She waved. "Your graces are as hollow as your callousness. I know full well what your feelings are, and you know mine. When you've had time to consider how fair I've been, then I'll listen to your regrets."

He bore himself back to his own room more frustrated than ever. There was a mote in his eye, and Grandmamma would not remove it. Neither would Otto. Nor would Ute. That left Anna. And she seemed to be ghosting farther into the background each day.

In blanching sunlight with a spring profusion bursting all around, Jimmy Pelt was buried. His sister, located in New York, stood small and dry-eyed next to Gerta, who prayed unrelentingly to the crucifix around her neck. Detlef was a mask. Anna, Kurt noticed sadly at graveside, was so confused she crossed herself backward.

No, he could not go to his aunt.

THIRTY-ONE

Heavenly wrath poured out of the sky and the shoppers on both sides of the street scurried for cover looking white and naked. Skelote could barely see out the windshield. The lightning was a blue-white rinse alternating with gray, closely dogged by thunder. The thunder reminded him of the hounds at the Hauptmann place, which was where he was going now.

The lane into the compound was a shallow stream, and the fir trees rasped the fenders and doors like the brushes in a car wash. He caught a single glimpse of the shuttered chapel in a flash of lightning, and then he left the car and made for the steps of the house. The hermetic clamminess of the porch welcomed him in its embrace. Skelote paused. The steady hiss of rain washed out sounds. He only sensed movement within the house, as if it were withdrawing, receding, closing up; but in a moment the screen door nudged slowly open, and the old matriarch's voice floated out, somehow complemented rather than curbed by the storm.

"Come in, Lieutenant."

He swiped a rivulet off his brow as he stepped softly across the threshold. "You've had your share of tragedy this year, frau, and you don't need a lot of bureaucratic nonsense hanging over your head, so I thought I'd come out and get this over with."

"Tragedy is an old boarder in this family, Lieutenant."

She gestured and he sat down opposite in a wicker chair with mauve cushions.

"You know, I never came out here about Mr. Hauptmann's heart attack, but I always wondered about that hide-a-key box with the baby aspirin in it."

"Like all of us, my son was getting more and more absent-minded as he grew older."

"Then his medicine was in the same kind of box?"

"Yes. Exactly right. He didn't want to mix them in the same container, because they looked similar. The aspirin was for arthritis."

"Funny he didn't keep them in the original containers."

Her face reaggregated into the sinkhole eyes and puckered moue. He had the feeling that this was where the house had gone, inside her somehow.

"Did Mr. Hauptmann know that the Nitrostat had to be kept in glass in order to remain effective?"

She blinked with interest. "Really?"

"That's what the doctor said. No metal or plastic containers. Tightly capped glass."

"Whose doctor?"

"His doctor."

"I see. You think that means something, then. Well, I can tell you about the glass. But as for the metal, I don't think Martin knew. He was afraid of breaking the glass. That may sound irrational, but artists of the caliber of Martin sometimes develop an eccentric rapport with their medium."

"Guess I haven't known many artists."

"They do indeed. My son had a phobia about breaking glass. In his art it could mean the loss of a priceless treasure. So much depended on precise handling. He simply refused to carry any sort of glass unnecessarily."

It had the quirkiness of truth to it. Skelote's poker face softened. No one could have forced Martin Hauptmann to use hide-a-key boxes. "What about the aspirin?" he asked just to be thorough. "That usually comes in a plastic bottle or a tin."

"Martin took five or six a day. He bought them in large plastic bottles, too big to carry around in a pocket."

"Yeah. I guess that's it. Frau, you're a saint to put up with me, and here I haven't even got to the other thing. God, that was awful. Anytime you want me to stop, just invite me to leave, will you?"

The room brightened with a timely flicker from the storm, and the windows trembled. A mantel clock seemed to tick slower.

"Let us talk about the other *thing*, Lieutenant."

"Well, I don't know if there's going to be an insurance settlement, or any legal action, but they always come looking for the police report, frau, so I'd better nail everything down."

"Nail away."

"Well, I was wondering about those hounds. Not that I'm a dog fancier or anything, but I didn't know they were that vicious. What kind were they?"

"I believe they were mostly Irish wolfhound."

"Wolfhound."

"Guard dogs, trained to protect."

"Did you train them yourselves?"

"My other son trained them."

"Detlef? That his name?"

"Yes."

Skelote nodded. "I hope his arm is going to be okay. He certainly paid a price."

"We'll all bear deep scars over this."

Skelote gave it a moment's reverence. "I guess you need protection out here. Dogs might do it."

"Stained glass seems to be a high priority among thieves these days, Lieutenant. A good twenty percent of our orders are replacements of this type. But tell me, is there any doubt about Jimmy Pelt's death being accidental?"

"Frau, my profession is all about doubting. If someone didn't doubt, people would get away with murder. It doesn't mean anything unless a crime has been committed."

"You must have been lonely for crime here in Padobar before these murders," she imparted with a crone's chuckle and her hoary brows went up. "It's gotten to be a habit, all this doubting."

Skelote grinned fixedly. "You're some lady. You should be an analyst."

"And you should be Irish."

Skelote smiled and stood. "My apologies for the imposition, frau."

He went back into the storm and brooded with it as he sat in the front seat of his car fogging up the windows. When the lightning flashed, he could see the chapel, and if it hadn't been for the rain he might have asked to have a look inside. Where were the dogs when Pelt had opened that door? If they had rushed up the stairs at him, why hadn't he at least backed outside? If not, why had they waited until he got to the cellar? And how had this Detlef restrained them? Both at once? It would have made more sense to pull Pelt out of the cellar, wouldn't it? If he took one dog out, the other would have had plenty of time to ravage. But he would know that. He would pull one hound out of the cellar, let it go, and then get the other one. Maybe he had. Maybe he had rounded them up afterward.

Details.

When you walked through it, you got most of them straight. The rest were just things you couldn't explain. Either you fit them to a crime or you conceded the world was full of quirks. Skelote couldn't fit them to a meaningful crime done in a meaningful way. The world was full of quirks. The stained-glass studio was a quirky place. It had recorded a couple of quirky deaths. He wasn't settled about it, but he wasn't really suspicious either. Whatever was wrong here, it had nothing to do with the string of killings county-wide.

So he would butt out.

He wiped the windshield with his cuff and started back to the office. And all the way, it rained like God needed a good cry.

THIRTY-TWO

THE SUN DRIED out the compound, summoning vines up from the earth and over the sheds, higher by the hour it seemed, while the trees leafed out extravagantly and the catbrier tracked aimlessly across the flagstones. By contrast, the buildings looked shrunken and withered. It wasn't just the damp or the rotting roofs or the weathering screens but something internal that had snapped. Kurt saw it, smelled it, tasted it as he stood on the pockmarked sidewalk. His eye took in the warped horizontals of the eaves, the rusted sprinklers, the cowering supports of the disused arbor intimidated by bushes, and saw in them something resigned and fatalistic that went beyond the shock of death.

"Ah, there you are!" Gerta called from the corner of the shed.

In that light she looked like translucent wax over blue rivers of blood. His eyes escaped to the much clasped crucifix that hung outside her collar.

"You got out of the house before I could speak to you," she said, and the purring sound was back in her voice. "Are you avoiding me?"

"We got up so late this morning. Besides, I wasn't hungry."

She gazed aloofly at the orange in his hand. "And are you very busy now?"

"No." His thumbnail skated over a patch of brown on the otherwise bright fruit.

"Good. Because I want you to take family communion tonight."

His eyes climbed quilelessly to her face. The word was misspoken, she should have said *confirmation*.

"Communion supper," she went on, "celebrated like the Lutherans, except that the symbolism goes back further to incorporate pre-Christian traditions. As a rule, only confirmed members of the family may attend."

"I don't want to be in the way," he murmured a little sarcastically.

And to his total surprise, she stepped forward, then resolutely slapped him across the face. He found himself caught in the harsh intensity of a Valkyrie's eyes, blunted by the stone determination of an ancient face.

"I'm making no concessions to you," she said. "The burden of seeing this generation through has fallen to me. I want it known that all the family under my wing participated in this communion dinner—*all* the family! You'll present yourself suitably dressed at ten o'clock in the living room. For two hours before that you must remain upstairs, where you will pray either by yourself or with Ute. Do you understand? And one more thing, have you ever had dreams about the craft or the family . . . as it was? Any . . . recollections that you thought were real but couldn't explain?"

It was precisely what had happened to him in the attic that day, but he shook his head, fearing exclusion.

"It has happened—once or twice—that the shock of recognition severely unbalanced family members who weren't already confirmed. If you are prone to such glimpses of the past, you might find yourself suddenly flooded with disturbing insights during the service. In that event, I wouldn't force you into this."

Her dire tone prodded him to tell the truth, but he saw the door closing again. "I want to take part," he said.

He stood for a long while after she was gone, scratching at the bruise on the orange and listening to an insidious breeze that had suddenly begun circling the compound.

Never had he been so full of misgivings. The question about his previous intuitions should have been answered candidly, but it was too late now. He couldn't risk discrediting himself. Gerta thrust him briefly into preparations just before eight—"Please put the extra leaf in the table, Kurt"—and then he was politely banished to his room.

"Pray," she had said. About what? He faced the crucifix above his bed, knelt self-consciously. Through the wall, Ute's vespers made a drowsy murmur. Grandmamma had said he could pray with her, but he knew what would happen if they got close in a bedroom for two hours, communion sanctification or not. Though the way she was going at it, it might not have mattered what he did in a room with her. He found it unbelievable that she would keep it up for the whole time, but after some forty-five minutes it seemed likely she would. The sheer weight of so much piety perplexed him. God was for him an omnipotent father figure with a distinctly German character whose dictums were brief and whose understanding was independent of words. By nine o'-clock he was trying to listen to Ute and God through the wall. Then he went and sat in the window.

Out on the grounds the shadows of trees raced together like closing teeth. There was no sending him to Chartres this time. Whatever there was to see this night, he was going to see it.

Presently Ute's filibuster yielded to the thud of dresser draw-ers. Nine-forty. Silence hemmed him in. The room grew hot. He heard a tap next door. Gerta's voice. Seconds later his own door re-verberated lightly. Wiping his sweaty palms, he opened it to his grandmother.

Her fingers lifted swiftly. "Renounce the inventions of man," she said as she stroked laterally across his brow.

He felt something clinging there. *Ashes.* "I renounce . . ."

". . . the inventions of man."

He glimpsed Ute in her doorway. ". . . the inventions of man."

"Now come to communion. You are an obedient grandson after all. And a handsome one in a suit, eh, Ute?"

Ute's eyes shut out the suit in meeting his, and there was an utter candor there that did indeed quicken his pulse.

A pair of ordinary candles subdued the room as they de-scended the stairs. Red wine from the *Kunstschrank* hung sus-pended in thin-stemmed goblets like a ruby glue, the china swam with yellow crescents, a score of utensils lay like commandos around the steaming center dishes. The candle holders were glass and very old. Kurt was sure they had been in the attic among the other arcane pieces of furniture. Beneath them was a tablecloth he had never seen before. Though it was partially obscured by the many dishes, he thought it was a textile version of a grisaille win-dow complete with apostolic figure in the center. Under the image was a motto scripted in an unfamiliar alphabet whose letters seemed to be all variations of the letter "M."

The sickly viridescence that had haunted the family's faces since Jimmy's death warmed in candlelight to a wholesome bronze, except on Anna where a layer of powder and the smear of ashes across her brow gave her the absurd look of an aging geisha.

And then there was Detlef.

Stealing glances, Kurt suddenly recalled the vivid tatter of a man who had arrived soon after Martin's funeral. What had happened to the murky, bloodshot scleras, the persistent cough? How had the bloated, dissipated flesh hanging round his throat tightened into strong cords? When had the gray-flecked hair turned black as ebony? The ruddiness and the pallor had evened out to a breathing, bloodless marble, somehow moist. In the shadows of his lips, Kurt caught the gleam of healthy, well-formed teeth.

"Perhaps Kurt has noticed the Germanic runes in the motto," Gerta was saying. "Why don't you translate for him, Otto."

Otto tilted his head. "It means 'God through ecstasy.' "

"Much of what has survived in family lore is written with those characters," said Gerta. "Magic was and still is an irrational path to God. And at least as successful as most, I might add, because it doesn't try to come to grips with God intellectually, but through faith and *sacrifice.*"

She gave him a moment, and he saw in the earnestness of their faces that they wanted a sign from him. He smiled wanly.

"Shall we begin?" Gerta's fingers pinched the cross around her neck, then moved to the stem of the wineglass. "This is my blood, the universal blood that I have given you and which flows back to me. Blessed be he who wills it so before I come. Drink and be warmed by the river of life." She brought the glass to her lips, and they all imitated the ritual. "Let the act be consecrated to the heart." Returning the glass, she dabbed her mouth on a corner of the linen napkin.

Detlef then passed his plate to her right, which she filled from the steaming contents of a silvered casserole. Kurt smelled lamb and gravy. The helping went back to the left. In this manner each was served on a plate that everyone had touched. When they all sat in the rising vapors of the gravy, Gerta spoke again:

"This is my body, the universal flesh that corrupts on the rock and germinates in the earth. Blessed be he who sustains the earth. Eat and be one with me."

With knife and fork, she cut a dainty morsel and chewed. All followed. Subdued ring of silverware, gentle stroking of china.

Kurt sucked gravy off a chunk as he turned it in his mouth. It was sweeter than usual—because of the wine, he thought—but a searing pain suddenly shot through the roots of his molar. His searching tongue identified the tang and texture of metal. He spat, and a dull clink emanated from his plate. Everyone was craning to see, but Kurt didn't notice. He couldn't. His eyelids were fluttering and the sanity was draining out of him, because the chunk of chewed flesh that had fallen bore the dusky blue imprint of a snake's coil, and across it was a raised pink streak, like a scar. Faint with horror, he recognized Jimmy Pelt's tattoo.

"This is my body . . . eat," Gerta's voice droned, and far into the night that liturgical murmur reached him, until his painful dry retching became chill sweaty nausea and Gerta was able to decipher his trauma.

"It was a packing stamp," she insisted, changing the cold cloth on his brow, "just the meat inspector's grade. You could barely see it. How could you think otherwise?"

And on she went, talking him down from the heights of madness to a vapid valley where he was led by the hand like a will-less child. And the metal, the shrapnel Mackey had told him was in Jimmy's arm? Through uncontrollable shudders, his heaving voice conveyed that doubt.

"A pellet, of course," she crooned in her syrupy grandmother's voice. "Someone shot the animal, that's all. It's not the first time I've found a pellet in a store-bought cut."

Pellet, pellet . . . Pelt.

She soothed him until he was outwardly sound again, then carefully asked if he thought he might have had a shock from the sudden recognition of the past, as she had warned.

Was the past so terrible, he wanted to know.

There were elements of taint that might repel him even more greatly than his delusion of the past few hours, she said.

Like Detlef?

Her brow constricted at that point, and she looked into him for a long time. Yes, she admitted finally, like Detlef.

She left him then, assuring him he was better; but he knew the crimson cracks of a lava-seamed mountain were gurgling inside him. And when the magma erupted, he feared he would have no control over it.

THIRTY-THREE

THE SKULL SESSION began when Skelote called in Catherton, Charlie Hegan, and Frank Dewey. Hegan, besides being unable to keep call codes straight in the patrol car, suffered periodic deafness but was the most dogmatic man in the department. Dewey had been known to fall asleep at a red light and to fabricate reports, but he had a gift for linking the essential points in a series of leads. Catherton, who had once stopped a funeral procession on suspicion that the driver of the hearse held an expired license, added zeal.

When no one looked like they wanted to go first, Skelote asked, "Have you gentlemen been introduced yet?"

"I don't see why we bothered with this," Dewey grumbled. "We're not New York City. We all know there's nothing new."

"Except that some sick prick out there keeps pumping blood over this county faster than the blood-sucking reporters can lap it up," Skelote said, and when Hegan cocked his head as if he were trying to hear but having difficulty, he added, "Don't pull that on me, Charlie."

"Not much to say, actually," Hegan sighed. "I checked out the spikes and the railroad ties from the Russell thing. None reported missing from local track in the county. Don't mean much, though. Unless there's a real interruption in a line, nothing gets reported. And spikes are always missing. All of that stuff could've come from any of seventeen equipment depots within a hundred square miles. Or it could've been lying alongside a right-of-way somewhere left over from a previous repair or waiting to be used." He paused, drumming his fingers, drumming up thoughts behind his bulldog eyes. "I checked with the lab, too. Concentrations of the preservative used in the ties were almost identical between the ones used on Russell and the ones used on the crucifixion in Trinity. The Norse Chapel one was different. Could've been a different batch run through the preservative in the same depot or maybe different depots."

"That means our boy planned ahead for the Trinity crucifixion the same time he planned Russell's," said Dewey. "Also means he didn't plan the Norse Chapel one then. He had to restock for that one."

"Maybe, maybe not," Hegan replied.

"What're you talking about, the ties were different, weren't they?"

"He means maybe the murderer just ran out," Skelote said. "He could've picked up the first bunch lying by a siding and there weren't enough for three crucifixions."

"Bullshit, he pieced the crosses together, didn't he? What are the odds he ran out with just enough for the second cross? Why wasn't there some overlap of lumber one way or another?"

"Would you have left lumber like that lying around after using some of it for a crime?" Hegan posed, pointedly calmer than Dewey.

"What the hell do you think he did between crosses one and two?"

"I think he picked it up in the same place—alongside a track, like Jack said. He knew there wasn't enough left for a third cross, so he went somewhere else then."

Skelote was smiling faintly. They weren't bad for a bunch of amateurs who hadn't done much more than herd drunks and write traffic citations most of their careers. "What about the bolts?" he asked Hegan.

"Superior Screw Machine Company, East St. Pete. They supply half the sun coast. Could've got 'em at any hardware in the county. And all three crosses were pieced together with them. He used a lapped joint to make the ties into single beams that were long enough. Fit them with a handsaw. No pencil marks, but a good fit anyway. The bolts were even on center."

"Sounds like a carpenter, or a tradesman."

"A tradesman would've used a table saw."

"Bullshit," Dewey reentered the fray. "Maybe he didn't want to invite his friends and relatives to see what he was doing in the basement. Maybe he took it out in the woods and he couldn't find a half-mile-long extension cord. Maybe he don't have a—"

"He used a post-hole digger for the holes," Hegan said. "And I walked a lot of track looking for pulled spikes, mostly near crossings. But no soap. He only needed a few anyway. Not likely we'll ever trace those." He paused, then modulated politely: "What have you done on this, Dewey?"

"You said half of what I was gonna say." He threw a pencil onto the table, palmed his hair. "All the physical evidence connects up. I'm looking at the murders county-wide, and it comes down to a lone psycho with a real hard-on for blood. His victims are special: the way they die is special, the fact that they're white is special, the fact that they're all males is special, for a while it looked like old age was special, but not no more, and I got a feeling there's something more here than just race. This guy revels in the dying. They all die slow. It's like the Dark Ages. He takes them out like a medieval torturer. Okay, maybe some of it is racial. Maybe one of the crosses is a slap at the K-cubed, but not that St. Andrew's thing. Not that upside-down business in Norse Chapel. This guy's a religious whacko or a satanist."

"The St. Andrew thing was because the victim's name was Andrew," Hegan monotoned. "Maybe he has a perverse sense of humor."

"I'll buy that, I'll buy that. He's a savage with a sense of fate. And he knows his victims' names. He knows their habits, their movements, their moments alone. He probably stalks them. And he's intelligent. All these different methods, you'd think he'd leave a clue big enough for the techs to find. And there's no pattern to the timing. Except that there *is* no pattern."

Skelote clasped his hands on the table. "There are two kinds of crime, basically. The ones that serve a legitimate need—'I want that money, I want that woman, I have to kill my enemy to survive'—and the wanton wasting variety that satisfy some abnormal human need. But even the second kind have a pace to them: our boy gets all excited under a full moon, or at least he gloats for a while over his victim. The other extreme is the binge, and that takes place in an afternoon of shooting at cars or hostage terror and the like. Our boy seems to fall in the middle. He isn't taking much time to get his jollies, and he isn't pacing himself either. It's almost as if he's trying to meet a deadline or a quota."

Catherton brought up the blood samples. "Maybe he thinks he's a vampire."

"The guy's a corpse-raper," Dewey opined. "*That's* how he gets his jollies."

Skelote unfolded his hands. "Are you done checking out Russell, Catherton?"

"There wasn't anything else."

"Pathology says they got a call from Russell's brother-in-law looking for his body. The caller pulled the pants off that little bleeding heart in the lab, and she sang the whole opera for him."

"Could've been a reporter," Hegan said.

"Yeah, that's what I thought. Here we go with a big Sunday edition splash about all the victims, epitaph and tears stuff. But maybe Dewey's right. Maybe we got some kinda corpse-raper."

"Hell, he had the corpses to begin with," Hegan said.

"True."

"He could've hung on to them until he was done with whatever he does."

"True."

"Maybe he don't have a mausoleum to store them in," said Dewey. "Or maybe he just couldn't cart 'em off from the scene of the murder. I mean, shit, he took the trouble to crucify three and all, could be he needs spectators or just didn't want to wait around for the dying."

Skelote slowly unwrapped a piece of gum. "If he took the bodies every time, what would we be working on?"

"Disappearances," Dewey answered.

"Right."

"And a lot of leftover crosses."

"Right."

"And spilled blood."

"We'd be doing a lot of searching," Skelote said. "A helluva lot of searching for missing men. I think this sicko doesn't want us to search that hard, because he's in the area. He's spread the murders all over the county because he's right out in the open. If we search hard enough we're gonna find him in a green and white house with a picket fence and a garden right in the middle of one of these towns."

There was a reflective pause, and Skelote broke up the session on that note, saying he would check out the Russell thing.

"Get somebody from Cyril's Institute on the line," he threw at Janet as he sauntered into his office. He rummaged for a pen on his desk and came up with three more sticks of gum, all of which he disposed of in his mouth.

"Cyril's on one!"

He picked up the phone. "Lieutenant Skelote, Padobar police."

"Dean Borkowski, Lieutenant. What can I do for you?"

"The corpse of a Caucasian male, name Andrew Russell, was donated to your medical school a week or two ago. It came out of a pathology lab in Marlo County. We have reason to believe someone may try to claim it—may already have, in fact—and that's what I'm calling to find out."

"I'm having trouble hearing you, you'll have to repeat that."

Skelote pulled the phone away from his ear to stare at it, put it back. "Can you hear now?"

"I can hear, but it sounds like you've got a mouthful of waffles."

Skelote flattened the gum into his cheek. "I'm trying to trace a body, and I want to know if anyone has been asking about a certain corpse that went to your med school."

"I'm not at liberty to discuss this."

"Discuss what?"

"What you want to discuss."

"Sounds like you've had a problem already."

There was a moment of indecision. "If this is a prank, I assure you you'll all be expelled when I get to the bottom of it. And if you've got the body, you'd do very well to let it be found by the authorities."

"I'm up to my ass in dead men, Borkowski, and I want to know about Andrew Russell's fucking body!"

"Very well. I'm going to assume you are who you say you are. The cadaver you speak of was stolen a few days ago. The Anatomy Building was broken into through the roof and the body taken out through a damaged exit. It's all in the hands of the St. Petersburg police, for whatever that's worth."

It was worth a lot. Almost as much as the autopsy report Skelote received by telephone just before he went to bed. This one was about the ax murder in Norse Chapel, courtesy of Captain Alby, N.C.P.D. The victim, Matt Matherson, had a needle mark over the heart. When he finally fell into a fitful sleep, Jack Skelote dreamed vampires.

And at five past six in the morning, it started all over again. "The honor of your presence is requested, sir," night dispatcher, Fay Larson, enunciated slowly into the phone after he picked it up. "It's a *five*, as in *murder* . . . numero cinco. Are you receiving? Three-nineteen Northline Road. The name is John Kemper."

"I'm en route."

He hung up, buried his face in the bivalve of his hands. Light beat against the wrinkled shade. Last night's comforts were this morning's debris. He skirted a pair of bottles and the leafy wrapper from a quarter pound of longhorn, kicked into his trousers, shrugged a shirt over his shoulders, and struggled with his socks. The denizen in the mirror wore a popcorn face—white and puffy.

He lied to it. "I hate cigarettes," he said. Then he put on a pair of brown shoes that weighed five pounds apiece.

Half a mile out of Padobar, he caught the swell of cars and people at the Kemper barn. The big attraction was a black, oily machine shaped like a miniature locomotive. Its upright, nipple-nosed cylinders chained to one end, flecked silver and green, were propane tanks. And the black swathes on the grass were tar. The barn was not the usual type, peaked in a gambrel roof, but rather a cinder-block rectangle with a slightly sloped top that had to be retarred every now and then.

Skelote remained hunched over the wheel trying to pick out the novelty. He had never been very good at spatial relationships. The tar-encrusted curve of the boiler separated slowly in his mind's eye from the angles and bubbled planes of the rest. And suddenly he saw the smooth glistening nod of a jet black head and shoulder above the rim of the tank. He was not aware of getting out of the car, but then he was walking around the tar burner in an introspective trance, fending onlookers back with a limply raised arm. At one point he stooped and examined a heavy, tar-coated rod that lay on the ground.

"Anybody touch this?"

"Not since we arrived," Catherton said at his elbow.

"Talked to anyone yet?"

"There's a man in the house—Dale Kemper. Came home from work an hour ago and found this. He says it's his father."

"How the hell can he tell? All right, get the examiner, and move these people out of here."

"Sir, you don't suppose there could be something to the fact of his being black now, do you?"

"Black now?"

"You know, the racial angle. I mean, this guy has been *made* black. Like a tar baby."

"Catherton?"

"What?"

"Be on the lookout for Brer Fox."

The examiner arrived forty-five minutes later and took charge of the body. Skelote asked him to look for a needle mark over the heart when the tar was removed. He questioned Dale Kemper for a few minutes, requesting that he submit to more questions later when he felt like it, and went on to the station. For twenty minutes he sat at his desk methodically hand-printing a list:

Marcus Adler	Padobar	riding accident (?)
Steve Laberdie	Padobar	gravel slide accident (?)
Luke Sutter	Padobar	hung—suicide (?)
Paul Johnson	Cicadia	decapitated
James McIntosh	Palm Hollow	clubbed to death
Tom Dufferson	Cicadia	speared
Andy Russell	Padobar	St. Andrew's cross
Phil Gibbs	Trinity	crucifixion
Charles Torley	Norse Chapel	crucified upside down
Matt Matherson	Norse Chapel	axed
John Kemper	Padobar	boiled in tar

Nothing came together. Nada. And then Janet ambled past, handbag slung over her shoulder, glancing at what he had written.

"Calling all saints," she said. "That's very Christ-like of you. Good-bye, Lieutenant."

His eye fell again on the names as she wandered out. Saints? Oh, Lord. The Gospel. Matt Matherson, Marcus Adler, Luke Sutter, John Kemper. And the rest of them were mostly apostles.

"Janet!" he shouted so loud that she heard him at the far end of the hall.

She came back like she had all the time in the world, and when she got there he just stared into her face as if he hadn't meant to call her, as if it had just slipped out.

"Did you have an attack of loneliness, Lieutenant?"

"How would you like to do me a favor?"

"Do I sound enthusiastic?"

"This won't take long. Come in twenty minutes late tomorrow."

"What is it?"

"I want you to go to the library and get me a book on martyrs. Something that tells how the most famous ones died."

"What's the matter, Lieutenant, didn't the librarian ever show you how to use the card file?"

She was back in a quarter of an hour with Foxe's *Book of Martyrs,* a very old edition of an older text. What he wanted emerged from the first pages, a synopsis of saints and martyrdoms. A blueprint. Skelote reduced it to his own shorthand:

St. Paul, Nero beheaded; St. Thomas, pagan priests of Parthia ran him through like Dufferson; Andrew, crucified at Edessa on a cross set up like an "X"—St. Andrew's cross; Philip, crucified (regular way) at Hierapolis, Phrygia, A.D. 54; Matthias, they stoned him before he was beheaded.—but Matt Matherson had been axed.

Then he found the name of Matthew, slain with a halbred in Nadabah, Ethiopia. One of the two James mentioned—James the Less—had died at the hands of the Jews at the age of ninety-four,

brains dashed out with a fuller's club. Skelote's accidents and suicide required little imagination to interpret. St. Mark had been
dragged to pieces, as had Marcus Adler; Luke was supposed to
have been hung; and St. Stephen had been stoned to death. Steve
Laberdie's gravel pile was probably an easier way, thought Skelote,
wishing he had taken Harry Wagner to the mat over the issue of
an autopsy. He would have to get a court order for an exhumation
now.

The sheriff's department didn't have any of this. The accidents were his discovery. And John Kemper's demise. They didn't
have that yet either. Kemper had fared worse as a surrogate than
the real St. John. According to the book, St. John was the only
apostle to escape a violent death, after miraculously surviving a
cauldron of boiling oil. And then Skelote saw the leftover name.
Charles Torley. He thumbed the synopsis. No St. Charlie. It was St.
Peter who had been crucified upside down. In Rome by Nero.
Frantically he rifled his desk, withdrew the sheet on Charles Torley, and read with satisfaction: Charles *Peter* Torley. Herschel
Kalb's profile of a religious four-eight slid comfortably alongside
his suspicions. It beat the "tar baby" theory all to hell.

Next he juxtaposed the locations. But except for the religious
sounds of Trinity and Norse Chapel, there seemed to be no pattern. He went back to the names. There were others, candidates for
future murders, maybe. The martyrdoms were ghastly. Under the
general persecutions of Nero, Christians had been sewn up in animal skins and worried to death by dogs. Others had been dressed
in shirts stiffened with wax, tied to axletrees, and lit on fire in
Nero's gardens.

And what about the book itself?

Skelote examined the card in the back pocket. It was possible
that the killer had used a copy of it; it was possible that he had

used this copy. Due dates were all over the card. He made the necessary call to the library.

"Once it comes back I throw away the slips, Lieutenant," said the librarian. "You can't imagine how many little scraps of paper pile up on my desk. Sorry."

After all the frustrated leads and untraceable clues, Skelote felt a breakthrough was near. And then he had his last revelation of the morning. The *overt* crimes had been committed out-county. But the first ones, which were made to look like "accidents" and "suicide," had happened in Padobar. Did that imply that this was the killer's base of operations? The killer hadn't expected the accidents and suicide to be traced, so he didn't bother to go afield for those early crimes. *He might be here, he might be right here,* Skelote groaned inwardly.

Apprehensively, he began a telephone campaign that started with Chief Wiggins of Trinity and ended with Captain Alby of Norse Chapel. Only Lieutenant Dickerson in Cicadia could recall a violent accident in the past year in his town, but it had involved a painter who had fallen thirty-five feet from a scaffold in plain view of a busy intersection. When Skelote hung up the phone for the last time he felt as though the killer were in the room watching him.

THIRTY-FOUR

IT WAS HEALING in the warm sun streaming through the windows for Kurt to abandon himself to sluggish morning currents, but beyond that refuge was another tide—vast, deep, persistent. He stood waist deep in its gray swirl, looking back into the night and his grandmother's face, filled with thoughtful energy. He got all the way out of bed, but dizziness forced him to sit down on the edge of the dresser. Time milled about him for a few giddy seconds and got back in step with his breathing. A sparrow flashed to his window, flinched, was gone. Nudging himself erect, he went to the sill. Except for the kitten passing down the drive with mincing steps, the grounds looked empty.

He pulled on blue jeans and crossed to his door. The house felt and sounded abandoned. That was good. He didn't need to face anyone this morning.

Downstairs looked like downstairs—no runes, no apostolic tablecloth, no glass candle holders. They were letting him compose himself.

And then he saw through the front window that the studio

door was open and a ragged pennant of flame was unfurling inside.

He watched to see how high the flame would lick, and when it stayed contained, he sauntered onto the porch, the drive. There was movement next to the flame now. Someone was waiting. For him. The vulnerable parts of himself were under interdiction to remain numb, but the atavisms of an inner person glided forward. In the doorway he paused.

"Come in," said his uncle. The voice, like the face, was now fully resurrected.

Kurt took three more steps to within a foot of the workbench. The flame spanked out of a crucible there fed by coarse sheets of paper. Jimmy Pelt's sketches. He could feel the heat.

"Are you better?"

"Yes."

Detlef added another sketch to the pyre, and the glow leaped up his rugged face. "What's bothering you, nephew, is it our little fights?"

"No one seems to mind how cruel you are."

The cold chisel laugh lodged in the rafters, and the wizard arc of a grin was repeated. "My son hates me, my niece despises me, my sister-in-law fears me, my mother questions my every move . . . but my nephew thinks I'm too popular. God preserve me from overconfidence!" He poked at the fire with a pointel, offering another sidelong glance. "Anything else?"

"You took me to Chartres a long time ago. I wish I knew why."

Detlef stirred the final ashes in the darkening studio, turning his attention to a row of bottles filled with pigments.

"I took you to Chartres because it represents the difference between God and man, your heritage of divine knowledge and the deceits of the churches. You saw the glass, and I told you what it represented. I showed you good and evil in the pictures . . . and magic. Do you remember the story of Hermogenes? In all that delirium of glass I picked out the exact line of truth and fraud for you. You were too small, of course, to understand the details, but you should have felt what I wanted you to feel. Instead you were ashamed. When I brought you back to Ursa after Monika's second confirmation, you wouldn't tell her where you'd been for weeks afterward. That's why you've never been a member of this family. Because you felt ashamed. Like Adam and Eve."

Lethean tides drained away on a stone floor Kurt could clearly visualize. There was more; his uncle was leaving the important thing out. "What happened in the crypt?" he asked evenly.

Detlef suspended the mixing of pigments long enough to shoot him a look of quiet scorn. "I see you didn't block out everything. The crypt, then. One of the biggest. Literally and figuratively the foundations of the place. It was built on a Druid shrine, like most cathedrals. Built and rebuilt until no one remembered anymore. Like the architecture itself, its dogma changed—the great sarsens into small cut blocks, the simple passion of man for God into a great absurd bureaucracy of worship. Can you understand the immortal travesty of that? To snatch God away from the living homage of man and entomb Him in the abstract coffins of books and vestment shrouds? The venal few have stolen God from man and man from God." He was facing his nephew, a bottle of frothy black pigment in his hand. Only the embers of Pelt's sketches heightened the shadows of a Gothic face. "I showed you the exact points of truth and fraud down there, too. Do you remember yet?"

The Lethean ebb was a mere hot trickle now.

"You kissed the one spot," his uncle said. "And on the other . . ."

. . . a hot trickle over the stone floor that deeply shamed a little boy acting on his uncle's insistence.

"You urinated," Detlef finished.

As simply as the removal of a splinter, that innocent truth eased out of Kurt's mind, and with it a barb of guilt that had grown to adult size on the tip of a childhood arrow. He was startled to find himself crying.

"You son of a bitch," he said in embarrassment.

"Because I made you pee or because I made you cry?"

"Did my mother know?"

"What difference would it have made? She would have understood, if she had known. Which is more than I can say for you. Sad that you again miss the whole point of it. You weary me, nephew. Isn't there enough insight in you to remember and understand anything?"

"Maybe it's because I've never had second confirmation."

"You would have by now, if it hadn't been for that little reaction then. I thought last night that you might have had a breakthrough."

"I do remember some things," he said through a slow procession of tears.

"Do you? I doubt it. Besides failing your instincts, you've proven yourself a sneak and a liar—"

"I do remember!"

Detlef took four even steps to the window, jerked the shutters open. "Do you remember this?" He held the pigment bottle to the light, and Kurt saw that it was not black but deep claret.

THIRTY-FIVE

"ANOTHER ONE, JACK." Chief Wiggins's voice sounded like a scratchy seventy-eight against the backdrop of midday confusion in Trinity's station house. "This one was tied to an axle shaft in a garbage dump and lit on fire. No age yet, but definitely male. If he ever was white, he's black as soot now. We're looking for a gas container."

Skelote sat lax and sweating in the quiet torpor of his office, one hand already cleaving through the pages of Foxe's ghoulish history to the short account of the general persecution of Nero, A.D. 67. *Axletrees . . . Christians tied to axletrees.*

"Stop looking for a gas can and check the ground for wax drippings, Daryl," he droned dispassionately.

"Wax drippings?"

"The man's clothes were soaked in wax. He probably had a biblical name and went to church regularly. And when the autopsy comes back, if they don't find a puncture wound in the heart, I'll kiss the examiner's fat ass."

"Did you get Kemper's sheet yet?"

"Yeah. A hot tar kettle, about four hundred fifty degrees, but he'd been tapped before that."

"You've got such a hot hand on the M.O., Jack, why the hell don't you tag me a profile?"

"Put out an APB for Emperor Nero, Daryl."

"What's that supposed to mean?"

"Never mind. Just check for the wax and the puncture and let me know if I'm right. I'm following up something, too. I've got a meeting with Judge Wanamaker at four over a court order for an exhumation. If I don't get it, there's gonna be one helluva grave-robbing spree around here."

Released from the sweaty suction of the phone, he remained lucid-eyed in his chair. If the human body was three-fourths water, Skelote figured to lose a hundred and sixty-two pounds today. He had discovered the killer's operating manual—Foxe's *Book of Martyrs*—and rational conclusions to a barely finite equation of horrors were due.

Here.

In this chair.

At this desk.

He had actually cleared the desk, and the mountain of paperwork that had always confronted him was now on the floor alongside the file. A half-dozen more pens had been glimpsed in the uprooting—like glistening black and blue pupae discovered under a rock—and already these had burrowed into eternity elsewhere in the office.

The liquid crystals of his watch said 5:46 in glowworm segments. Time for the bloodhound to go for bones.

▪　▪　▪

JUDGE WANAMAKER'S SIGNING of the order was a mere formality. Skelote already had a shovel in the trunk of his car. As it turned out, the cemetery insisted that the grave should not be disturbed except by their own workmen. It added another delay on top of the one needed for the examiner and the deceased's ashen-faced brother to arrive separately, but two wiry types jolted up in a ten-year-old convertible just about dusk.

Armed with tools and lights, the assembly weaved through the hoveled twilight of the parched burial ground, past heavy pastel gravestones in the older section to the crisply chiseled white squares of the newer. There they bunched together, sidling, reading, then at last filing around the gravesite whose marker read STEVEN LAWRENCE LABERDIE.

A pair of shovels and a long-handled spade were tossed down. One of the diggers began edging the plot with an ice chopper, the other nudged a withered wreath off the catafalque hump with his foot, glancing at the same time toward the brother of the interred. When that end was cleanly hemmed, he jammed the spade under the sod and began to pry. The flayed surface was rolled into four helixes resembling green frosted cake-rolls.

Skelote stroked two fingers over his lips, missing a cigarette. This thing they were doing had better turn out right. He didn't mind Harry Wagner screaming like someone had stepped on his balls—that was a plus—but if he was wrong about this, where did it leave him? The examiner had expressed doubts. What embalming hadn't removed, a feast of bacteria had. Laberdie's family was upset and uncertain. No exhumation order had been granted in Marlo County since 1948. If it wasn't for public unrest over the murders, the whole proceeding would have been summarily dismissed in chambers.

Shrugging off the pastry chef delicacy with which they had handled the crust of the grave, the workmen stripped to their waists and fell into a rapid, loose-jointed pace. A silver religious medal, penduluming and dancing around the taller one's neck, became the point of fixation. Skelote sidled around the grave, the caretaker glanced at his watch, Jason Laberdie scratched his elbow, the examiner lit a cigarette.

"How come there's never any birds in cemeteries?" Skelote undertoned. "Squirrels, rabbits, but no birds."

"Too many angels to bump into," murmured the examiner.

"I trust you'll take care of this as quickly as possible, Lieutenant," Laberdie said. "The sooner my brother is interred, the sooner our family will get over the shock."

The man was a good four inches shorter than anyone at the grave but still managed to look down his nose at them. He was the kind of guy who would sue if the exhumation turned out pointless. Skelote didn't care. But it wasn't going to turn out pointless.

They stared into the grave, half-dug, absorbing the chill. The workman's medallion silvered the abyss. A breeze stirred damply out of the cypress swamp to the north, and a fireball embered the clouds that dogged it to the horizon. Two birds twittered in a brief westward chase that Skelote didn't hear. He was busy arranging the battery lanterns so that their swaths vectored into the yawning hole. It was close to the moment. They all pressed forward. The examiner got rid of his cigarette without anyone seeing how; Laberdie itched but didn't scratch.

Where the hell was the coffin?

The workmen were easing their shovels into the rich loam, anticipating contact, and now they too seemed surprised. In alternate surges they stabbed deeper. Once again the shovels came up full—black irregular loads that collapsed in a rain on the mound. It went on. Shoveling night out of a hole.

The body wasn't there.

The grave was empty.

One of the diggers raised his shovel in both hands and drove deep. This time there was a ringing sound. Faint. More lyrical than metal.

Skelote grabbed a lantern, pouring light into the hole. Something bright glittered—a sliver of red, a shaft of blue—like refracting jewels. The shovels skated over it, catching black ridges.

"It's glass," the caretaker recognized.

Reaching down between spread legs, the diggers grasped rectangular edges and raised a full-length stained-glass window.

THIRTY-SIX

UTE SAW THE stricken look on Kurt's face when she returned from shopping and knew he had talked with Detlef.

"It's not fair to keep him out like this," she complained to her mother. "He should be allowed to have second confirmation. Did you see him when we drove up? He's wandering around the compound like a little lost boy. He can't take this much longer—"

"Exactly. He can't take it, Ute."

"Don't you think he deserves an explanation at least? Uncle is tormenting him."

Wearily, Anna shook her head. "Look how he reacted at communion supper when he choked on . . . when he thought the lamb was human flesh."

"But that was nonsense!"

"And what about the Passion-Kirche? Do you think that will be any more palatable to him?"

"It will be if he remembers."

"But he doesn't. Not nearly enough."

"Neither do you!" she accused her mother. "You don't have

any ancestral memory. Why is that different? Or is it only different if you're never tested?"

Her shrill sarcasm flustered Anna into stammering that no one had ever questioned her commitment, least of all a daughter, and that she was one of the few who was ever trusted with the history after marrying into the family.

"Were any of the others ever tested?" Ute persisted.

Anna closed her eyes for a moment, then opened them in a fixed stare. "This has nothing to do with Kurt. If you want to know, he was ashamed as a child when Detlef took him to Chartres, and he's still ashamed. He's blocked the ancestral voice inside himself. That's why he's not ready. Because he's ashamed, Ute."

"It's Uncle Detlef who makes everyone ashamed, not the past."

"You never understood your uncle," Gerta gruffed from her chair across the room.

Ute colored slightly. "It's not hard to understand sadism."

Gerta looked through her granddaughter. "Nature's creatures always overdo their instincts, or they don't survive. The lowest slug is prolific, the flower spews its germs on the wind to guarantee its existence. Place a gopher in a wooden box and it will continue to try to dig. The salmon and the eel make pointless journeys into the past, the lemming rushes to extinction. All echoes of a purpose. Detlef is a genetic pawn in the evolution of the family. And if his purpose echoes, you must tolerate it."

"You make him sound like he isn't free to do what he wants."

Gerta moved to the sink and slowly ran a glass of water. "None of us are as free as we think. Today we do this, tomorrow that, but in the space of a lifetime, a subtler, more farsighted purpose is served. Our genes aren't subject to free will. And there are moments in life when one's genes do take over. You should know that, Ute. Isn't it exactly that kind of farsightedness which keeps the family intact?"

"Then you're not going to tell Kurt anything?"

"We all want Kurt to have second confirmation. Try to see that. And watch that your heart doesn't interfere."

A dusky blush poisoned Ute's anger as she marched out the front door.

"She's as strong-willed as you," Anna observed behind Gerta.

▪   ▪   ▪

ANNA CHAIN-SMOKED. Anna drank wine. Anna's hand shook when she poured the wine she drank. *Never tested, never tested . . .* Ute's words burrowed deeper. Not in her most intense nightmares had she imagined this would fall to her generation. She did not want to be tested. She did not want her daughter to see her tested. Anna wanted out.

And Detlef was the only way.

He would be in his cellar again. Finishing. What did she have to lose? She had lost her husband. She had lost control of the studio. She was losing her sanity. It was too late to stop the crimes, but, oh, how she wanted to miss the rest! And she would. She must, this instant before Gerta returned and weakened her resolve.

Leaving the remaining groceries on the counter, she began to cross the compound. "Oh, Martin, Martin, forgive me for not being able to see it through," she prayed.

This was her major sin. Betraying Martin. He had lifted her from the nightmare of her youth. Hers had been a family riddled with addictions, depressions, estrangements. Martin's complete dedication to his gentle art and a dynasty as strong and independent as the one in her fantasies had rescued her from her own warps. And as she had gradually learned the depth and scope of Hauptmann survival through the millenniums, through all its many names, through the rise and fall of governments and civilizations alike, it had thrilled her with its invincibility. That was why she had been trusted. It was the mirror image of her own insecure and vulnerable roots. For once she had picked the winning side. She would have excused its horrors even if they had been under way at that moment. The greater good was obvious. And when she underwent the isolation and fasting in preparation for second confirmation, she had thought then that no direct descendant with those dominant genes for family characteristics could have been more sincere, more staunch in their loyalty than she. Loyalty. It was bondage after all. And even though it still seemed right in eternity, she knew she hadn't the makeup to endure its unfolding in her own generation. Not without Martin.

There were no hounds to sound discords this time. White and fresh and radiant, Detlef was already facing her when she came down the cellar steps. Next to him, the reds still glistening wet, was a stark portrait of John the Baptist's head on a platter. She felt like a child about to tell a lie to a very stern and perceptive parent.

"I came about Kurt," she said.

"Did you?" he replied brightly.

"This is all happening too fast for him."

"Really?" He got up, circled her.

"Much too fast. It isn't the family's custom to push its members—"

She was wearing a cotton dress with a drawstring bodice, and he reached out and plucked the bow.

"You tried that already," she attempted to say in a bored voice, but the last word trembled.

"Did I?"

"Kurt isn't ready. You can see that . . . can't you?"

He hooked his fingers over the elastic top of the dress and stretched it down over her ample breasts, his knuckles brushing her nipples.

"Some things just have to happen when they happen," he said.

She struggled against his inane assault, but he grasped her waist in both hands and bowed to her breasts, slowly sucking each ruby crest.

"I thought this family thing . . . only happened after persecutions," she managed breathlessly. "I thought . . . there had to be hate."

"Hate enough for me in Germany," he murmured in the hollow of her flesh, and she felt his resonance clear to her backbone.

He was taking everything. He was family, he was man. Her husband's brother. Millenniums of evolution were reaching out to bind her; but she wasn't from the past, she was now, and she had prerogatives.

The hose lay curled up in the tub, still attached to the threaded faucet. Her right hand fumbled for the valve, spun the gate open. Immediately the hose became tumescent, erupting in her hand. She aimed it directly into his eyes.

He fell away, pawing his face. She thought he looked like the Wicked Witch of the West, gaping and melting in his own puddle. But she had the sense not to wait, and throwing the hose at his head, she hammered up the steps and back across the compound to the sanctity of the house, where no one waited.

Except Gerta.

▪ ▪ ▪

SEVEN MILES OF therapeutic cycling were required to rid Kurt of the giddy fear Detlef had inspired. He pedaled slowly on Melton Road, feeling angry, then hurt, then scared. In a damp glade hemmed by palmettos he got off his bike and cried. Afterward he stumbled feverishly around a mud-rimmed pond, unconsciously snatching at weeds and slapping insects. When the little ritual was over, and his emotions had subsided to a dull ache, he meekly raised the racer and began the journey back.

Another forty minutes passed before the chapel tower came into view. For the first time he noticed that all six windows on the east face were shuttered. It was after seven o'clock, he judged by the premature dusk of the sheltered compound. Up the steps he strode, expecting to find a room full of questioning faces. But Gerta, Anna, Otto, and Detlef were missing. And there on the sofa, as if keeping vigil, sat Ute.

She was dressed very simply in a white blouse and black slacks, the ebony crucifix outside her collar. Her red hair was burnished in the single lit bulb of the three-way pole lamp that shone also on her face and throat. She gave him a deeply meaningful look that dispelled all doubt between them, but which he recognized contained the same element of hopelessness as before.

"I told Grandmamma that I thought you should have second confirmation," she said.

"And . . . ?"

"She said no." Without turning her head, she followed his progress to the stairs. "Kurt. Did you ever finish those books in the attic?"

"No."

"Did you read about Walpurgis Night in Germany, or the Haberers?" He was leaning over the rail above and behind the sofa. "The Haberers were a kind of peasant court of vigilantes. They began in the Middle Ages and still sometimes pop up in small villages. They hounded us for centuries. They hated us because we were different. I thought you might remember . . ."

"The way you remember?" His steps came back down one by one.

"Yes. That way." She clasped her right wrist in her left hand. "I believe you do remember some things. How people hated us."

"Who?"

"The Romans?" she half asked, limply gesturing with the clasped wrist. "They hated us because they said we were Christians. Some of the Christians hated us because they said we were idolaters. There were always enemies. Sometimes it was a government, sometimes just a village. Very few generations escaped. Later it was the Inquisition. The family was large then and spread all over Europe. In a matter of forty years we came close to extinction." Her look pleaded for him to remember. "Even in America. The Puritans hated us."

"Why?"

"The Puritans rejected all embellishments they thought kept them from contemplating God. In our case, stained glass."

"And the others? Did they hate us because of men like Ultrich Guenther? Like Detlef?" He knelt suddenly, one hand on the sofa. "Do you know what he's doing? Do you know that he's probably a murderer?" The words tumbled out of the fear-ribbed cavern of his subconscious, a revelation to himself. "All this secrecy, and . . . and the hounds killing Jimmy, and my gloves down by their cages, and today . . . today he showed me a bottle of blood. He's making glass with it, Ute. I don't know why he's doing it, but I'm almost positive he's the killer they're after. I think he's put bodies or parts of bodies in the cistern out by the chapel. That's why the hound disappeared. He dragged it into the woods and strangled it because it was barking at the cistern. What's worse, Grandmamma's protecting him, because he's her son. I don't know what she's told you, Ute, but you've got to wake them up to the truth of what's going on."

And then he stood unnerved before the meter of Gerta's descent. She cast him burning looks despite the difficulty of the stairs. And when she got close enough, she wagged a finger under his nose, preaching hoarsely: "What do you know of any murders? What do you know of Detlef? What do you know, for that matter, of Ultrich Guenther?"

Her face hovered close beneath his, and he barely had time to notice Anna and Otto standing grimly in the two doorways, before the vortices of Gerta's eyes drew him wrathfully in.

"Listen to me," she said in a voice as cold as the croak of a frog. "God is ambivalent. The paths to worship are ambivalent. And the forbidden ones are the shortest. On such a journey the approach is sudden. The participant seizes the divine prerogative of life and death, and in a blinding moment of exhilaration spans the chasm to God. Do you think the mystical brooding of prayer and all that nonsense of incense and hymns is anything less than that leap done in slow motion? It's the same. It's passion. Passion, Kurt. That which we had in the beginning before knowledge. Remember the runic motto on the cloth? *God through ecstasy.* Faith and sacrifice, I told you we believe in. What did you think sacrifice meant? In the beginning it was *human* sacrifice. God has no better purpose for us. The judgment on one who is sacrificed is lucky indeed. Only cowards and the unworthy resist that holiest of values, the faithful perserve."

She paused to let him understand, but he was clearly horrorstruck.

"*Remember,* child . . . remember how it was. The family has survived in its craft of building and rebuilding its church over the generations. The Passion-Kirche. Remember? And every so often the catalyst comes, the tainted one who serves his purpose, like the salmon and the eel and the lemming . . . Detlef, child . . . Detlef."

He grew faint, dimly collecting the faces about him. Sad faces. Ute crying. Otto, jaw clenched as if holding something down. Gerta shaking her head and taking one of his arms while Anna, absolutely ashen, grasped the other. They bore him out of the house, sagging, unable to walk. In the cold, thick gloom he heard his aunt's accusation: "He won't recover from this, Gerta, he's in shock!" But as they passed up the drive in a somber knot, Gerta continued to school him, as though racing a deadline. This was the night of the Passion-Kirche, she kept saying.

The shutters on the west face of the chapel were gilled with intense light—crimson, blue, gold. At the chapel door he moaned and had to be supported by Otto. Slowly that portal swung open, revealing, as they pushed him forward, a swarm of colors. Leaning backward into their arms, he was thrust one rubbery step at a time into the torch glare. His face, convected by waves of shock, was mottled, his lips twitched, his gaze slipped from wall to floor to ceiling with demented ease.

The chapel plan of pews and altar had been restored, but something in the added facades of rough-hewn beams along the walls gave a mock cathedral appearance to the simple structure. It had an illuminated nave such as no civilized worshiper had ever seen, towered over by ghastly stained-glass windows. The texture of these was unspeakably grim: twelve martyrs depicted in their utmost agony, each in the manner of death. And each was represented within the lattice of lead cames and glaze by his own putrid corpse! They hung in bas relief, a mingling of medium and reality, preserved with all the ravages of dying. There could be no question of Detlef's skill, despite the monstrous twisting of the craft. Each cadaver or remnant was subtly bound in came-work and sprayed with some lacquer or fixative so that the glass itself seemed to swell and conform. Neither Anna, Gerta, Otto nor Ute raised their eyes. It was left for Kurt to take in the hideous gallery of surrogate martyrs like a leering lunatic to whom sense and sensation were one.

—except for the fourth window on the east wall, which pictured the rending apart of Ignatius by animals at the hands of the Emperor Trajan. That window brought a tremor of recognition, and the young man silently convulsed at the one-armed Bishop of Antioch: James Ignatius Pelt.

"He doesn't remember," Gerta's voice hummed behind him. "He just doesn't remember."

Detlef took him by the arm then and led him to the altar, or rather where the altar should have been. Kurt saw a huge block of smoky glass. It took a fraction of a second longer for his dull gaze to penetrate to the man inside, crouched forever in grotesque prayer. That was all he could tolerate. His eyelids fluttered and he drifted to the floor. The Reverend Peter Torley, late of Norse Chapel, crucified upside down, was now the altar of the Passion-Kirche. Peter, the rock of the church.

▪   ▪   ▪

WHEN KURT CAME to, it was dark and his head was aching. Gritty stone met his hand in two planes—a floor and a wall. All around was the pungency of propane gas. He was in the chapel cellar. For a moment he thought he heard the vapid rasp of a saw cutting through thick timber. But then the short dull notes changed rhythm, taking on human complexity. It was a chant, a litany. Mausoleum murmurs from the chapel above. They were still up there, and that terrified him. His holy family. Soul deep in ancient *sacraments* that defied moral order. And he dared not reason further, because hadn't he accepted the explanations before he understood the consequences?

To be sure, the transcendental exhilaration of defying cardinal laws was utterly beyond him, but the shock of stained-glass eyes pouring out through shredded flesh had awakened something, some satyr composed of opposing moralities. He was Kurt Nehmer and he was Kurt Hauptmann. No matter. It was too great an abomination for the one, too great a guilt for the other. He had to stop it.

The two of him.

Crawling blindly along the wall, he found the corner, then the stairs, and finally, as his hand groped up and down stones, the light switch. The effort of standing and the brightness sent another wave of illness through him. The clutter of cellar objects swam surrealistically in the effluvial vapor around the gas cocks. He caught sight of the friction lighter for the welding torch that Detlef had used on the lead cames. Next to the easel in the corner were cutting implements and a bottle of kerosene. A pile of rags lay nearby. Only one question remained.

Which Kurt would survive?

The gas cocks went on first, hissing like snakes climbing toward the chapel; then he got the friction lighter. He would have to sit at the top of the cellar stairs to avoid being overcome by fumes while enough accumulated. Dragging one of the rags free of the pile and lifting the bottle of kerosene, he crept up the steps in the dark.

There he sat as he had the day of his imprisonment, allowing his head to roll back and forth against the door. It gave a little. The hasp had a stick in it as before. Shakily he raised himself and pushed until the door yielded a slim opening. The friction lighter was one of the thin wire kind, shaped like an oversize safety pin with an angled head. The stick came out on the first try.

Tears streamed hotly down his face as he tottered around to the front of the chapel. The chain and the padlock were still there. Detlef's voice was a roar as Kurt drew the chain through the handle. A moment later the doors rattled. Then came the oscillations of uncertainty. Kurt stood there as if frozen by that uncertainty from the other side of the door. And however long it took them to smell the gas, that was how long he remained suspended. The murmur rose then. He began to back away as if the cries were pushing him. And in a sense they were. Because the family he had sought so desperately to enter in was leaving him forever. Leaving him at his instigation. They were all shouting and pounding before he reached the corner. That was the only detail he would later recall.

For a long time he sat on the grass waiting for the chapel to fill, while hell arrived by degrees inside. He was still in shock, still flickering on the border of extinction and denial. The cries of the imprisoned five were rending. Each poignant intrusion brought another wave rushing reflexively over his mind, smoothing the shores of sanity. That was *not* Ute's broken calling of his name just then, and her frail hand could *not* possibly fist the door like that.

Aunt Anna was *not* sobbing hysterically. So many lies, so many tricks. It was Detlef. All Detlef. Whatever he touched became tainted and therefore no longer what it had been. You couldn't let yourself believe in illusions, in voices, around Detlef.

But the insanity outside was nothing compared to what reigned within. From the moment the chain rattled through the chapel-door handle, Detlef changed, as if he knew in an instant that the demiurge of centuries now vested in him was doomed. He blackened the torches, hurled Bibles at the high stained glass. It was a tantrum that mystified the others at first. They exchanged looks in the failing light, fired questions. Was it Kurt who had locked them in? Or an outsider? The authorities would have stormed in immediately, Anna thought. Gerta suspected an old enemy: the malevolence of hateful neighbors. Otto and Ute had no judgments at all but watched with rising alarm as their uncle guttered the torches. And then, as if sight deprivation keened other senses in the ensuing total darkness, they caught the first whiff of gas. It tasted flat initially, a vague recognition lost in the limbo between palate and sinuses. Then it grew to where it was no longer a meandering thread in the air, but an oppression, like a chloroformed rag clamped violently over the face. And that linked the door chain to the cellar and to Kurt . . . and to betrayal. Such a long chain. Gerta reacted with a great bottomless cry, Otto with rage, Anna with fear. Ute was the last to let go of denial, calling Kurt's name, pleading. The screaming and the gasping and the futile ramming of furniture that followed brought chaos. Each sooty breath in the darkness deepened the sense of purgatory. In the end, the Hauptmann clan regressed down millennia to collide like soulless animals in the primordial void. No, Kurt's visions could not compare to the Goya-like nightmares within.

And that was how he rose at last beneath a moon and stars frozen in place, unscrewed the cap on the kerosene, stuffed in the rag, sparked the end with the friction lighter, and smoothly underhanded the thing down the stone steps.

The divine thunderclap threw him some twenty feet backward and echoed agelessly down the road to Padobar.

THIRTY-SEVEN

IT LOOKED TO Skelote like the bombed-out shell of a German church after World War II. They had moved the bodies—what they could collect. Six. One, amid the scrabble of a fractured block of glass, had a little gold cross that had somehow resisted the heat and the flame. On the back was printed:

PETER
God's rock

Thirteen murders, he was figuring now. He hadn't counted James Pelt before. The scattered human carrion would add up to twelve more. One for the altar, one for each gaping window frame. And he knew where the eleven stained-glass originals were plus the one they had dug up. With court orders he would have the graves opened. The saints themselves had replaced their namesakes, grave by plundered grave. He probably never would be able to piece it all together. Unless the boy could help. They had taken him to the hospital in a state of shock, still clutching the oddly grotesque black crucifix. Someone named Mrs. Mackey was going to foot the bill. She had said that the boy wasn't part of the original family but just worked there.

"Lieutenant."

Skelote walked slowly to Catherton's side and stared down into a cistern whose heavy wooden cover had been partly moved off. The decomposing remains at the bottom shimmered iridescently.

"Looks like those two hounds he shot on top," Catherton said.

Skelote made fists inside his pockets. "Looks like a lot of stuff. Bring it up."

Too bad he had been so damn slow, he thought. You sat at your desk until all the pieces fit, and even the ending became academic. But he had made too much of Martin Hauptmann's heart attack, and maybe the realization of that had slowed him down. Ironic that the trail led precisely back to the Haputmanns after that initial red herring. He took out a cigarette. No use trying to be better than he was. When you saw this much death, you were glad to be alive. He thought he should be glad to be alive from now on. One woman didn't care for him, another did. Life was like that. He thought maybe this evening he might stroll over and bang Nora Sandles, and then tomorrow, come hell or high water, he was going to take his granddaughter, Brenda, to Disney World.

January 30, 1977

Dear Mother,

I didn't know. How could I know?

They tell me I didn't speak or close my eyes for eleven days. That's hard to believe. It feels like it happened a few hours ago.

Last night I stood at the window and looked

down the road to the family cemetery. It was burning. I guess that was what brought me back from shock. I remembered then. All those burnings in the past. This morning, before Mrs. Mackey got up, I went down there and looked. The stones are scorched and the grass is burned off. Somebody must have poured gasoline over the graves and lit it. So now I've seen the hate, and it terrifies me . . .

Ute is buried next to Anna and below Gerta. Otto is next to Detlef. But they survive in me. And I have the gift now, because I remember everything. In a way, I've also had second confirmation. So I'm coming home as soon as I can arrange it. With the money from the sale of this place we should be able to open a new studio. It's going to take a long time, but everything the craft needs to survive is inside me.

Faithfully,